Eternal

The Queen's Alpha Series, Volume 1

W.J. May

Published by Dark Shadow Publishing, 2018.

This is a work of fiction. Similarities to real people, places, or events are entirely coincidental.

ETERNAL

First edition. January 15, 2018.

Written by W.J. May.

Also by W.J. May

Bit-Lit Series
Lost Vampire
Cost of Blood
Price of Death

Blood Red Series
Courage Runs Red
The Night Watch
Marked by Courage
Forever Night

Daughters of Darkness: Victoria's Journey
Victoria
Huntress
Coveted (A Vampire & Paranormal Romance)
Twisted

Hidden Secrets Saga

Seventh Mark - Part 1
Seventh Mark - Part 2
Marked By Destiny
Compelled
Fate's Intervention
Chosen Three
The Hidden Secrets Saga: The Complete Series

Paranormal Huntress Series
Never Look Back
Coven Master
Alpha's Permission

Prophecy Series
Only the Beginning
White Winter
Secrets of Destiny

The Chronicles of Kerrigan
Rae of Hope
Dark Nebula
House of Cards
Royal Tea
Under Fire
End in Sight
Hidden Darkness
Twisted Together
Mark of Fate

Strength & Power
Last One Standing
Rae of Light
The Chronicles of Kerrigan Box Set Books # 1 - 6

The Chronicles of Kerrigan: Gabriel
Living in the Past
Staring at the Future
Present For Today

The Chronicles of Kerrigan Prequel
Question the Darkness
Into the Darkness
Fight the Darkness
Alone in the Darkness
Lost in Darkness
Christmas Before the Magic
The Chronicles of Kerrigan Prequel Series Books #1-3

The Chronicles of Kerrigan Sequel
A Matter of Time
Time Piece
Second Chance
Glitch in Time
Our Time
Precious Time

The Hidden Secrets Saga
Seventh Mark (part 1 & 2)

The Queen's Alpha Series
Eternal

The Senseless Series
Radium Halos
Radium Halos - Part 2
Nonsense

Standalone
Shadow of Doubt (Part 1 & 2)
Five Shades of Fantasy
Shadow of Doubt - Part 1
Shadow of Doubt - Part 2
Four and a Half Shades of Fantasy
Dream Fighter
What Creeps in the Night
Forest of the Forbidden
HuNted
Arcane Forest: A Fantasy Anthology
Ancient Blood of the Vampire and Werewolf

THE QUEEN'S ALPHA SERIES

ETERNAL

USA TODAY BESTSELLING AUTHOR

W. J. MAY

1

Have You Read the C.o.K Series?

The Chronicles of Kerrigan

BOOK I - *Rae of Hope* is **FREE!**
  Book Trailer:
  http://www.youtube.com/watch?v=gILAwXxx8MU

How hard do you have to shake the family tree to find the truth about the past?

Fifteen year-old Rae Kerrigan never really knew her family's history. Her mother and father died when she was young and it is only when she accepts a scholarship to the prestigious Guilder Boarding School in England that a mysterious family secret is revealed.

Will the sins of the father be the sins of the daughter?

As Rae struggles with new friends, a new school and a star-struck forbidden love, she must also face the ultimate challenge: receive a tattoo on her sixteenth birthday with specific powers that may bind her to an unspeakable darkness. It's up to Rae to undo the dark evil in her family's past and have a ray of hope for her future.

Find W.J. May

Website:
http://www.wanitamay.yolasite.com
Facebook:
https://www.facebook.com/pages/Author-WJ-May-FAN-PAGE/141170442608149
Newsletter:
SIGN UP FOR W.J. May's Newsletter to find out about new releases, updates, cover reveals and even freebies!
http://eepurl.com/97aYf

ETERNAL Blurb:

WHEN THE KING IS MURDERED, his only daughter, Katerina, must flee for her life. She finds herself on a strange and dangerous path. Alone for the first time she's forced to rely on her wits and the kindness of strangers, while protecting her secret at the same time.

Because she alone knows the truth. It was her brother who killed the king. And he's coming for her next.

Alone and struggling she finds herself an instant target, until a mysterious protector comes to her aid. Together, and with a collection of the most unlikely friends, the group must navigate through an enchanted world just as fantastical as it can be deadly. But time is not on their side.

With her brother's hired assassins closing in at every turn, Katerina must unlock a secret that's hidden deep inside her. It's the only thing strong enough to keep the darkness at bay.

Can she find the answers she needs? Will she ever take her rightful place on the throne?

Only one thing is certain...she's running out of time.

Chapter 1

THE GIRL STOOD AT THE window, staring bleakly into the world beyond. There was nothing but darkness as far as the eye could see. A land blanketed in shadow, a night without stars.

Only a single light penetrated the endless gloom. A flaming beacon shining on a distant hill.

Even from miles away, she could see its brightness. The wild flames stretched up into the heavens, lighting the countryside around them and flickering in her eyes. Even so far away it was impossible to miss, and even without anyone saying a word the girl knew exactly what it meant.

My father's dead. The king is dead.

The flames whipped even higher in the midnight breeze, and she took a sudden step away from the window. Her crimson hair spilled in rivulets down her chest, and despite the shadows all around her eyes shone bright in the darkness. Shimmering with the weight of a thousand tears. Gazing out the frosty pane of glass with a sadness that knew no words.

He was a hard man, her father. But he was her father nonetheless. And over the years, time had softened him. His children had softened him. He wasn't as hard as he once was. There was a lightness beneath the weight of the crown. At times, he seemed almost ready to smile.

"We've got to go, milady!" A sharp whisper cut through the silence, breaking the girl out of her spell. "We can't stay here anymore!"

The girl blinked several times, forcing herself back to the present, then turned to look at the cluster of frightened women standing at the foot of her bed. Despite the late hour, they were all fully dressed. It was an ingrained instinct, one that had travelled to even the highest levels of the land. If you wake up to a scream in the night, the first thing you do is put on your shoes.

"You're right..." She swept through the center of them, moving strangely, as if she was in some sort of dream. "I need to pay my respects to my father..."

The women exchanged a frantic, helpless look as she groped around in the darkness, reaching for her coat. Less than a second later an ominous rumbling shook the very ground they were standing on, followed by a series of distant screams.

"Milady, you don't understand." The bravest of the women stepped forward, reaching tentatively to catch her hand. "There isn't time—"

At that moment the door burst open, and the women fell back with a shriek. The girl looked up in a daze as a tall man strode into her bedchamber. A man who had weathered a hundred battles and had lived to see nights like this before. A man she had known all her life.

"The king is dead," he announced with no preamble.

Although the beacon had told them as much, the women gasped and clustered together. The girl merely glanced at the beacon outside. Her thoughts were jumbled and made no sense. A chaotic parade of random memories, nonsensical and ill-timed. Each one hurrying to replace the last.

This is the man who taught my brother and me to ride when we were just children. My father is dead. I wonder what kind of magic sets the beacon on fire. My father's dead. I must remember to tell the groom to have my horse saddled in the morning. My father is dead.

When he received no response, the man glanced nervously at the women gathered behind her. They shook their heads, at a similar loss, and he tried again.

"Your Highness...your father is dead."

Her eyes flickered up to his rain-soaked hair, wondering vaguely at the smear of blood on his face, before she nodded robotically, pointing back to the window. "Yes, I saw the beacon. I was just gathering my things to go pay my respects—"

"You don't understand!" A wave of panic tightened his voice, as if they were running out of time. "He didn't just die, milady, he was killed. Killed by a dagger to the heart. This dagger."

He reached inside his coat and pulled out a shining blade, pressing it firmly into her hands. A tiny jewel was missing from the left hilt, and a steady stream of crimson was dripping onto the floor.

For a moment, she simply stared. Then a jolt of delayed shock rocketed through her body.

...Kailas?

"No." She held the blade away from her body, as if proximity alone could fight back the dark truth that was settling upon her. "No, this isn't... it isn't true. I know what you all must be thinking, but it isn't true. It can't be."

The man bowed his head, staring down at her with unspeakable sympathy.

"It's the prince's blade, milady. And he used it himself. I was there."

She shook her head back and forth, letting the knife fall from her hands as she backed all the way to the window. "There has to be some kind of mistake. Kailas...Kailas wouldn't do this. He would never hurt our father—"

"He *killed* your father," the man interrupted urgently. "And he's coming for you next."

The room seemed to get smaller and smaller as her eyes zeroed in on the blade. She was there the day their father gave it to him for Christmas. He'd broken it the very same night. Smacked it so hard against a suit of armor that one of the jewels had fallen out of the hilt.

"You need to leave the castle, milady. You need to—"

"I'm not going to run!"

The words echoed in the room, strong and fierce, freezing everyone inside to sudden stone. They came from a place deep inside her. A place she was only just beginning to understand herself. But as the beacon flickered in the glass behind her, it was as if the flames had jumped inside her body as well. Shock and fear gave way to anger. Anger and a fiery resolve. A demand for justice.

"I will not run," she repeated, her eyes locking on her brother's bloodied blade. "The castle is my home. The throne is mine by right. I will fight for what is mine."

It was a rousing speech. But one that was ended by just a few simple words.

"Then you will surely die."

All the women in the room turned to look at the man for the first time. He was tall and strong—even for a knight. But tired. Tired in a way the girl had never seen before.

"Everything that's happened tonight, your brother has been planning for months." His eyes flickered to the door as the chaos and clamor engulfing the castle began to get closer. "The guards are dead. The nobles loyal to you and your father are away from court. You have no allies."

The girl shook her head, her crimson curls ablaze in the fiery torchlight. "But the answer can't be to steal away in the middle of the night! There has to be a way—"

"Katerina."

The name stunned her senseless, stealing the words right off her tongue.

Growing up as a member of the royal family, the rules of the court were clear: First names were reserved for family. *Only*. If anyone else dared to speak them, they would be put to death.

But death was exactly the game they were playing here. That's what he was trying to say.

"You *need* to run."

Their eyes met for a second more. Just a second, but it was enough to change everything. A wave of sudden resolve rushed over her as she dropped the fancy coat she was carrying and reached for a travelling cloak instead. The man nodded and rushed back down the hall—assumedly to buy her as much time as he could—while she turned to her ladies.

"You will not be coming with me."

A small outcry followed the words. As frightened as the women were, they were fiercely loyal at the same time. Proud to stand next to their mistress to the bitter end.

"What are you talking about?" The woman who'd grabbed her before made to do so again, unwilling to let her go. "Of course we're coming—"

"You all have husbands here at court. You have family in the village." Katerina shook her head, wrenching her arm away. "They'll use those people against you, and I won't have the blood of your families on my hands. You'll stay here and accept my brother's rule. I command it."

"But milady—"

"I *command* it."

The two women locked eyes for the briefest of moments. A silent, heartbroken exchange passed between them as they reached out and squeezed each other's hands. Then another explosion shook the foundations of the castle, and everyone sprinted out of the room.

The women ran one way. Katerina ran another.

Now that she was out in the open, away from the sanctuary of her private chambers, it was easy to see that things were not as they should be. The halls were lit with torches, not tapers, and hardly three seconds could pass before the stones would echo with a chilling scream.

Katerina raced along in the shadows, moving as quickly as she could. Since she couldn't be certain of who her brother had rallied to his side, she would be forced to trust no one. Forced to steal away from the castle and out into the darkened world beyond all by herself.

Just a few months after the most recent rebellion. When the people living in the countryside and villages would just as soon kill me as call me their queen. Perfect timing.

The sudden sound of footsteps made her freeze in her tracks, and her eyes widened with terror when she saw the tall shadows of armored men stretching up the wall. A silent gasp tore from her lips as she whirled around in a circle, searching desperately for a place to hide. All the doors were locked, and the hallway she'd been fleeing down stretched back for at least fifty feet.

I'll never make it! I'll never get back the way I came before they round the corner—

A sudden hand clamped over her mouth, and she choked back a scream. The torches blurred in front of her eyes, and the next thing she knew she was being yanked backwards into a hole in the wall. A hole that hadn't been there just a second before.

"Alwyn?"

She hardly dared to whisper the name, and sure enough, the hand tightened upon her mouth in fierce reproach. Another hand came up in front of them, waving quickly over the gap in the wall, and no sooner had the stones stitched themselves together than a contingent of guards rushed past.

They're going to my room. They're going to kill me.

Strangely enough, the sight didn't solicit any emotional response. Perhaps she was in a place beyond emotions now. Perhaps her body had gone into some kind of shock.

"She's not here!" a male voice shouted to the rest. "You, head to the tower. You, go and check the stables. Kailas says we're to bring her back alive."

There it was. Straight from the guard's own lips. Her brother was behind this. Her beloved twin had given in to darkness once and for all.

The hand restraining her disappeared and a flood of feeling rushed back to her face. She reached out a hand to steady herself, but just as she did the stones in the wall disappeared once again and she found herself stumbling out into the hall.

This time, she wasn't alone. A small white-haired man tumbled out beside her.

"Alwyn." She lifted her arms for an automatic embrace, like a child reaching for a security blanket. "I knew it was you—"

"There isn't time." The wizard's brow was knit with fear as he looked up and down the endless hall. "We must go back the way you came. There's a tunnel hidden behind one of the portraits near your room that leads out of the castle. It's your only chance at escape."

Escape. So even the castle sorcerer sees no alternative. I'm to live in exile.

She might as well have been speaking out loud. Ever since she was a young girl, the wizard had always been able to read her thoughts. It's what would make her such a good queen, he always said. The fact that she had nothing to hide. That she wore her emotions on her sleeve.

"Yes, dear one, I'm afraid escape is your only option at this time."

He was about to say more, when the sound of footsteps echoed suddenly from up the stairs, freezing them both in their tracks. They stood there a moment, hardly daring to breathe, before he gestured urgently up the hall.

"Come on, quickly now."

With the greatest of haste, they raced back down the stone corridor towards Katerina's bedroom, the hems of their cloaks swishing frantically over the floor. As the guards had already checked her chambers, they didn't run into any trouble. But just as they were racing past her door Katerina skidded to a sudden stop, compelled with an instinct she couldn't control.

"My mother's necklace," she panted, her eyes wide with terror. "I can't leave it!"

Anyone else might have just thrown her over their shoulder but, as usual, Alwyn seemed to understand. His magical eyes flickered towards her room before he nodded sharply.

"Be quick."

Like the floor itself was on fire, Katerina raced into her room. Only to come to another sudden stop. It had been empty when she left it, but it certainly wasn't empty now. All those women she'd told to flee and submit to her brother's rule, all those women who had grown up with her and Kailas since they were all just children... those women were lying dead on the floor.

It was as if her brother had thrust the blade right into her belly.

She doubled over at the waist, breathing hard through her nose, hands on her knees. They were stacked in a pile on the rug. Her mother's old rug was stained through and through with blood. Little trickles of it were stretching towards her across the floor, and she took a sudden step back. Convinced that if it touched her, she'd give up and join them all willingly.

"Milady!"

Alwyn's voice hissed from the corridor. Reminding her of her purpose. Reminding her of the need for haste. A hundred tears streamed down her cheeks but she forced herself to turn away, leaving the mangled bodies behind as she raced towards her bureau. She would grieve for them all in time. But to stop now would be tantamount to death.

Her mother's pendant was hanging where it always was. Shimmering innocently in the moonlight. Oblivious to the fact that the world was crumbling around it.

Katerina froze a moment, her eyes dazzled by the otherworldly glow. Then she snatched it off its hook and looped it over her head, stuffing it deep down under her nightdress.

The familiar weight of it was an odd comfort as she left the chamber of corpses behind and sprinted out into the hall to meet Alwyn. As was the heat. For no explicable reason, the necklace had always seemed to create its own heat. It burned comfortingly against her chest as she and the wizard took back off down the hall, coming to a sudden stop in front of a portrait hanging at the end.

"This?" Katerina asked incredulously, staring up in disbelief. "This is my escape?"

It was an old painting, one that had been commissioned when she was just three or four years old and had hung in the hallway ever since. A painting of the prince and princess posing together in front of the royal throne. Each child was holding onto a different armrest.

Alwyn gazed up at the painting for a moment, then shook his head with a sigh. "My dear, the universe is nothing if not ironic."

Another explosion shook the very foundations of the castle as he grabbed one side of the frame and pulled it with all his might. There was a quiet groan then the painting creaked open like a door, revealing the dark passageway just beyond. Both he and Katerina stared into the shadows with wide eyes before she took a step forward, and he took a step back.

"You're not coming with me?!" she asked in alarm, clutching the necklace.

He tried to take a step forward, then suddenly stopped—like a dog that had reached the end of its leash. "This is as far as I go, Katy. I am bound to the castle by the same magic that runs in my veins. I can take you no further."

...then I am going to die. Katerina shrank back in terror, but he grabbed her by the hand. A rush of heat sprang up between them before the princess jerked away, rubbing her palm as though she'd been burned.

"A simple spell," Alwyn panted, "and my parting gift. As long as the magic holds, no one will be able to track you. Head east. Put some distance between yourself and the castle. With any luck, the incantation will last until then."

Katerina paled, glancing over her shoulder at the shadows beyond. "And if it doesn't?"

He didn't answer, he simply took her hand. "Keep to yourself, and don't stop moving. You'll be a thousand times easier to find if you try to settle down. And whatever you do, never trust a shifter. They are loyal to the crown."

But I am the crown. At least... I'm supposed to be.

His arms opened wide, ready for the final embrace, but just as the two were leaning towards each other a sudden chorus of shouts exploded at the far end of the hall. Instead of embracing her Alwyn pulled away instead, shoving her roughly into the tunnel.

"*Run*, Katerina! Run until you can't run any more... then keep running!"

Just like that, the painting swung shut. Leaving her alone in the dark.

WHEN YOU LIVE IN A place all your life, there ceases to be any mystery to it. Over time you come to know every crack, every shadow. With a bit more artistic talent, Katerina was sure she could draw the castle by hand.

But she would never have known to draw the massive series of tunnels beneath it.

How can this all be here? And why did no one ever tell me? Do they all just not know?

She couldn't believe that Alwyn would send her down into the earth if there was a chance her brother could follow. And she couldn't believe that her father had known anything about the subterranean labyrinth either. Their castle had come under siege many times before. Never once did he send people down to guard the entrances to the tunnels. The entire castle must not have known.

Ignorance is bliss. This place feels like death.

After stumbling a while over the jagged ground Katerina slowed her pace down to a walk, wrapping her arms tightly across her chest. How it could possibly be summertime in the world above, she would never know. The tunnel was absolutely freezing, but not in a way that she recognized. Not in a way one could simply shrug off and soldier on. The cold seemed to have a life of its own. Creeping down off the walls and reaching through her skin. Entering her body with every shivering breath as it burrowed its way down into her very bones.

She wished she was wearing more than just her nightgown under her thick cloak. She wished that she had enough courage to light a torch, to fight the cold and guide the way. But the image of her murdered ladies flashed before her eyes, and all those thoughts were put to rest. Instead, she simply gritted her teeth and continued walking. She would come back out into the real world soon enough. And when she did, chances were she'd be longing for the tunnel.

Time ceased to matter. The outside world couldn't manage to touch her so far beneath the ground. Each breath was memorialized with a frosty cloud, and each step pounded to the rhythm of the silent mantra, looping over and over in her head.

My father is dead. My father is dead. My father is dead.

The only comfort she had was her mother's pendant, but even that seemed to diminish so far beneath the castle walls. What had once been a strong, pulsing light had faded to the burn of an ember, and the heat that had once kept her so warm had turned to bitter ice.

She shivered again and pulled the hood of her cloak up over her crimson hair. Any moment now, she would be coming up on the moon-drenched lawns that surrounded the castle. The cloak was a good start, but her bright hair would be a dead giveaway. No one else in the kingdom had hair of such an unusual hue. She was known for it far and wide. Like her mother before her.

Sure enough, no sooner had she thought the words than the ground suddenly rose in a sharp incline. She crept up the rough stone, careful not to make a sound, and came to a stop in front of a thick wall of holly.

Holly? There is no holly on the castle grounds.

Her outstretched hand froze just inches away from the pointed leaves.

No...but there is holly in the forest.

For the first time since awakening to the beacon, her face lit with the hint of a smile.

Alwyn, you're a genius.

Like a person emerging from a grave Katerina clawed her way through the thick underbrush, fighting back tears as the serrated leaves tore at her skin and tangled themselves in her hair. Her fingernails ripped to shreds as she battled for every inch of ground, staining the path behind her with smears of royal blood. It was exhausting work—and still, she was in darkness.

But then, just as she was on the verge of giving up, a sudden ray of light pierced through the branches, into the tunnel. Her eyes locked onto it hungrily, starved of its comfort for too long, and she redoubled her efforts. Just a few minutes later, she was standing on dry ground.

Shaken. Exposed. But free, nonetheless.

And that's when she heard them. Her brother's hell hounds. Racing through the woods.

"No!" Her hands clapped over the mouth, but the damage was done. Her gasp was barely louder than a whisper, but the dogs were meant to hunt and kill. They would surely have heard it.

Without a second thought, she took off at a dead sprint. Flying over the forest floor as fast as her feet would carry her. Running in a straight line, away from the sounds of the massive beasts.

She ran past the brook where Alwyn had taught her to fish as a child. She ran past the giant maple tree that she and Kailas had played under as children. One by one, her childhood haunts flew past in a moonlit blur. Each more fleeting than the last. Each one staying in her mind for just a fleeting moment before getting lost in the darkness beyond.

Would she ever see them again? Was this goodbye?

A bloodcurdling howl echoed through the trees and she picked up the pace. Leaping over a shallow ravine. Tearing her way through the blackberry brambles beyond. Her feet hardly made a noise as they skimmed over the mossy forest floor; fast as she was, she knew it was no use.

There was no escaping a hell hound once it was on your trail. The only solution was to hide.

Hide, and pray that it would never find you.

There was another howl as she scrambled up the side of a hill, and then promptly tumbled down the slope just beyond. She cracked her head against a giant hollowed-out log on the canyon floor then promptly crawled inside, staring through a crack in the wood with wide, terrified eyes.

Not two seconds later, a hound emerged. Bigger than a wolf. And far deadlier. It sniffed the wind, then let out a fearsome cry. A moment later, it was joined by its brother.

Romulus and Remus. Mythological siblings who turned on each other. How appropriate.

Together, the giant beasts searched the little canyon. The thick fur on their shoulders standing up. Their savage yellow eyes piercing the starless night.

A dark abomination of the animal world, hell hounds were bred in the shadows beneath the mountains on the outer rim of the kingdom. Nothing but bloodlust and destruction in their veins.

Her father had banned them outright. Anything that was born so far within the badlands wasn't allowed entry into the kingdom. But he could never manage to say that to Kailas, especially near the end. When the puppies had first come to the castle, their tiny fangs dripping with the blood of a freshly killed rabbit, her brother had been delighted. Since then, the trio had been inseparable. The beasts followed the prince wherever he went, dogging his every step.

The wind picked up through the trees and the dogs sat back on their haunches, noses pointed towards the moon. A feral snarl rumbled out of Remus' chest, curling his lips back from his teeth as he rotated slowly around and zeroed in on the fallen tree.

Katerina cringed away from the light, clutching her mother's necklace as she leaned as far away as she could into the log. One wrong move and the dogs would tear apart the tree like it was an unfortunate plaything. Her body would not be far behind.

As Romulus picked up another trail leading out of the canyon, Remus made his way over to the tree. Katerina covered her mouth with her hands, freezing in breathless terror as he lowered his nose to the peep-hole, his foul breath blasting into the hollow log. Another growl rumbled through him, making her heart stutter and skip, and as he opened his mouth—his monstrous fangs gleaming in the light—she found herself offering up a silent prayer.

If anyone out there is listening...please protect me.

He lowered his eye to the peep-hole and stared straight at her. Then he walked away.

Katerina's arms dropped to her sides in shock as both hounds took up the fresh scent and disappeared over the ridge of the mountain, vanishing with a final howl at the moon. She was shaking so hard she had to hold onto the tree for balance. And when she finally dared to emerge, the beasts were long gone and she found herself quite alone.

What? What the... What just happened? I could've sworn that...

The pendant glowed warm against her skin as she turned her eyes back to the castle.

"Alwyn."

It seemed his tracking spell had worked after all. Still, she wasn't taking any chances.

The second she was sure the dogs could no longer hear her, she took off running again in the opposite direction. The wizard had told her to head east, but at this point any direction would do. As long as it was away from the castle, it was fine by her.

So for the rest of the night, Katerina did exactly what Alwyn had told her to do. She ran until she couldn't run any more... and then she kept running.

It came in bursts—tapering off with exhaustion—then exploding out of her once more. Up one mountain, and down another. Winding through an endless series of trees. Wading her way across river after freezing river, dragging her body back up onto dry land.

By the time the sun peeked out over the tops of the trees, she was lost and disoriented. More tired than she could ever imagine. More shaken than she could possibly withstand. Cold and hungry, stumbling one foot after the other in a sort of bloodshot daze.

It wasn't long after that she came to the top of a grassy hill. Since she'd been trekking through mostly forested mountains thus far, she could only imagine that she had left the boundaries of the kingdom behind and was in one of the rural provinces that bordered their lands. She had never been so far from home before, and even in the state that she was in she couldn't help but stare at the picturesque beauty of it all.

Then she twisted her ankle on a loose stone, and went tumbling down the hill.

A thousand cracks and bruises later, she finally hit the bottom. But this time, when she rolled to a stop she didn't try to get up. The world around flickered and dimmed before she finally gave up the ghost and closed her eyes. Slumping lifelessly into the tall grass. Waiting for death.

"I REALLY DON'T THINK you should be poking her like that, Nixie. It looks like the poor thing's been through enough."

"Oh, what do you care? It's not like I'm hurting anything."

"Would the two of you just give it a rest? Now give her some space. Wait, she's waking up!"

Katerina's eyes fluttered open and shut as she slowly awakened to the world around her. A world that was drenched in sunlight and sprinkled with morning dew. Three bright lights were twinkling in the air above her, and she raised her head weakly, trying to focus.

"I'm just saying she doesn't look much like a princess."

One of the lights dive-bombed the other with a little smack. "Quiet, Beck! She can hear you!"

"Hello?" Katerina's voice trembled as she pushed onto her elbows, squinting painfully into the sun. "Are you...are you talking to me?"

A tiny voice squeaked a startled reply.

"Heavens, she can't even see us! I forgot, we're still small!"

There was a sudden burst of warmth as the three lights hovering in the air grew bigger and bigger, eventually lowering to the ground. It got to the point where they were so bright that Katerina had to look away. By the time she turned back, three little women stood in their place.

"It's a pleasure to meet you, Your Highness." The woman in the middle bowed, and the other two quickly followed suit. "My name is Marigold. This is Nixie and Beck."

Katerina scrambled back to her feet, staring with open-mouthed shock. "You're...you're fairies!" She had heard of them, of course, but such creatures weren't allowed anywhere near the castle walls. Truth be told, there were rumors that they had died out decades before.

"See?" Nixie's mouth curved up with a little smirk. "I *told* you we're famous."

Beck reached around and smacked her again. "Shut up!"

"Yes," Marigold replied, stepping forward, ignoring the childish scuffle, "we're fairies. And I'm very glad that it's we who found you this fine morning."

"Oh, yes?" Katerina took a step back, nervously pulling her cloak tighter. "And why is that?"

The fairy's eyes warmed to such a degree that her tiny feet seemed to leave the ground. "Because, dear princess...we're going to help you live."

Chapter 2

GROWING UP IN THE CASTLE, things rarely changed from day to day. Royal life was run by routine to such a degree that Katerina honestly couldn't remember the last time anything spontaneous had happened. It was a fact of life, one she'd never really minded before. But one that left her completely unprepared for the events of the last twenty-four hours.

"...which is when I said, of course we have to go! It's the summer solstice! Only happens once a year! But you know kelpies. Once they get an idea in their heads, they're impossible!"

Katerina nodded quickly, trying her best to keep up. Even though the trio of fairies had shrunk down to stand at about three feet tall, they were still making their way over the forest floor without the slightest bit of trouble. The princess, on the other hand, was struggling every other step with her dainty shoes and billowing cloak.

"Of course...impossible," she echoed faintly, wondering why exactly she was following the strange women into the woods in the first place. "And what exactly is a kelpie?"

"What's a kelpie?!" Nixie erupted into a high-pitched explosion of laughter. A sound that chattered her own teeth and made the flowering buds around them open into full bloom. "What's a kelpie, she says! And here I could have sworn that no one who grew up in that castle had a sense of humor..."

"That's *enough*, Nix!" Beck, the darker-haired fairy, sprouted little wings just to circle back around and kick her friend in the back of the legs. "Honestly, with you babbling on like that what's she going to think of us?!"

"Both of you, be quiet!" Marigold never even broke pace, keeping her eyes always on the path ahead. "Don't worry, Your Highness. We're almost there."

Katerina nodded silently; oddly enough, she wasn't worried in the slightest. Yes, she was on the run from her brother's paid assassins in the middle of the forest with nowhere to go. Yes, she was tired and cold, and hungry enough to consider trying to eat Nixie. But from the moment the fairies showed up in the meadow, a strange sense of calm had settled over her.

She turned ever so slightly to let her eyes flicker over the strange group, soaking in all the fascinating details with a curiosity she couldn't control. Back when she was just a child, there had been books in the nursery about all sorts of magical creatures. Fairies and nymphs, goblins and ghouls. She would look at the pictures for hours, her eyes dancing with wonder as she imagined the fantastical world outside the castle walls. When she got older, those books were not only removed from the nursery but were banned from the castle altogether. Along with all those creatures inside.

Alwyn was an anomaly. The only creature with magic still allowed within the kingdom. Most of the rest of the wizards had been killed off, too powerful for their own good, but the little mage had saved the life of the king while hunting in the woods. Ever since, he'd been welcome inside the castle walls. He was a protector, an advisor—later, a tutor for the royal children. But even so, there were some doors that were never open to Alwyn. And while the castle was the most beautiful gilded cage there ever was, it was a cage nonetheless. Despite his truest wishes, Alwyn could never leave.

"—you talk to me like I'm still a child!"

"—then stop acting like one!"

A little smile crept up the side of Katerina's face, and she quickly bowed her head to hide it.

These fairies were nothing like the ones in the books she'd read. The little twinkling balls of light that floated serenely over the meadows, coming to rest upon every flower. These fairies were like bickering school children. Always a second away from ripping out each other's silky hair.

"I said *enough*," Marigold reminded sternly, oblivious to the clusters of blossoms that sprung up in her every footprint. "Don't make me come back there."

Another secret smile. Another stolen glance.

Although they all looked about the same age, Katerina got the feeling that the other two had somehow been entrusted to Marigold. That she was responsible for them, come thick or thin. And although they resembled humans, albeit tiny humans, it was impossible to miss the whimsical differences that set the two species apart.

To start, the fairies looked like an explosion of color. Nixie had fire-red hair that clashed horribly with her bright yellow dress. Her eyes were a strange amber color that seemed to change depending on the light, and every time Katerina looked at her she seemed to have more and more flowers in her hair. Beck was exactly the opposite. Jet-black hair, vibrant green eyes, and an amethyst gown that trailed behind her on the leaves. She was clearly trying to be mature, but every time the little upstart beside her said something she couldn't resist jumping down her throat.

Marigold was by far the most dignified, but even she was painted head to toe with the fairy brush. Her soft golden curls arched in an unrealistic halo around her round face. Her sparkling blue eyes, while beautiful, were a shade Katerina had never seen. And her dress, wrapped with a golden band around her bulbous body, seemed to change length depending on where she stepped.

All of them were barefoot. None of them was remotely cold.

"Ah, here we are."

Katerina looked up in surprise as Marigold came to a sudden stop in front of a dilapidated shack in the middle of a clearing. The shutters were falling off the windows, the roof was sinking in with rot and mold, and the entire thing was blanketed in a thick layer of cobwebs.

"This is where we're going?" she asked in a low undertone.

Nixie bounced up and down, wearing a wide smile.

"Home sweet home!"

With the caution of one who'd been hunted through the woods by a pack of hellish dogs, Katerina followed them slowly up the front trail. She didn't notice the way the garden came alive behind them. The way the picket fence that surrounded the perimeter sprang up from pieces on the ground and linked itself together, shining with what looked like a fresh coat a white paint. It wasn't until Marigold lay her hand on the door that the princess realized things were changing.

"What the—"

She leapt a step back as the roof popped up into place, sending a layer of dirt and moss flying into the trees. A second later, the crooked shutters began realigning themselves, coming to frame two panes of glass that were sparkling clean. Like a little dance, everything that had been broken or foreboding about the little cottage fixed itself brand new—all under the orchestration of Marigold's guiding hand. By the time the fairy was finished there was even smoke rising from the little stone chimney, beckoning them all inside.

"There, that's better."

Without a backward glance the jovial little woman pushed inside, leaving the door open behind her. Beck was quick to follow, and Nixie gave Katerina a friendly push as she skipped inside.

"Like I said... home sweet home."

Katerina had to duck slightly to get through the little door but she straightened up in a hurry, gazing around the cozy cottage in wonder. It was exactly how she would have imagined it.

Overflowing cupboards stacked with dishes and pieces of china. Garlands of herbs and spices hanging from every corner of the kitchen. Three tiny beds sitting in a garden of flowers in the corner. And a stack of well-worn books piled on a stool by the crackling fire.

"It's...it's perfect."

She spoke without thinking, then flushed with shame as she realized there were tears in her eyes. As strange as it was, something about being in the happy little home made her suddenly realize that she had lost her own, and the pain of it was almost too much to bear.

Three pairs of hands shot out to help as she sank down onto the nearest sofa, covering her face with her hands and shaking with silent sobs. Her hands were still frozen and smeared with blood, and only now that she was off her feet did she realize that her legs couldn't stand another second.

"I'm sorry," she whispered, embarrassed to be falling apart in front of the kind women who had welcomed her into their home. "I'm so sorry. I don't know what's come over me—"

"What's come over you is that you've been trapped in a nightmare, dear one." Marigold stroked her hair away from her eyes, rocking her soothingly back and forth all the while. "I was surprised when the tears didn't start ages ago, back when we first found you."

"But why are you helping me?" Katerina was almost afraid to hear the answer. "I don't have any money with me. I have no way to pay you—"

"Pay us?" The fairy settled down in the chair beside her with a jolly laugh. "My dear, does it look like we have a lot of use for money? The way we live?"

Katerina's watery eyes again flickered around the little cottage before she shook her head.

"Besides," Marigold continued gently, "what kind of fairies would we be if we didn't help a frightened young girl all alone in the forest?"

"Bad ones," Nixie whispered helpfully.

Marigold closed her eyes with a grimace, then flashed the others a strained smile.

"Why don't you two make yourselves useful? Get our guest something to drink?" As they scampered off, she took Katerina's hands in her own. "At any rate, we might not live inside the kingdom proper but even we were able to see the beacon. And judging by the fact that you're out here, while your brother is in there... I'm guessing you've got quite a story to tell."

Fortunately, she didn't ask to hear it. All she did was give the princess' hands a gentle squeeze. A rush of warmth shot up between them, and Katerina looked down with a gasp.

Gone were the lacerations covering her palms. Gone were the cuts and abrasions lacing their way up her arms. It was as if she'd been wiped clean. Every scrape and bruise, from her toes to the crown of her head, had vanished without a trace, leaving only glowing porcelain skin behind. Even the fingernails she'd broken clawing her way through the holly had been magically repaired.

"How did you—"

"Drink this, my dear."

Nixie and Beck had returned, each one offering a different cup of tea. Only, it was a kind of tea Katerina had never seen before. A sweet-smelling concoction of both purple and blue.

"What is it?" she asked tentatively, taking the first mug.

"That one is for cold," Marigold explained, watching as she took a sip. "It's not something we fairies are highly aware of ourselves, so we keep some on hand for visitors."

It was like stepping into a warm bath. The second the bubbling liquid passed Katerina's lips, a wave of heat blossomed inside her. Starting in her chest and working its way out to her fingers and toes. Her fingers eagerly clutched the cup, and she would have gladly kept drinking forever if Beck had not snatched it back and replaced it after only a few heavenly sips.

"And that one is for sleep."

Marigold answered the question before Katerina could even ask it out loud, and watched as the princess stared uneasily down into the cup. The sapphire mixture sloshed back and forth, sending up a cloud of steam that made her sleepy just inhaling it.

"I'm not sure," she said quietly, nervous in spite of herself.

The fairies had treated her with nothing but absolute kindness from the moment they found her on the hill, and yet she found the idea of letting her guard down in a house full of strangers rather terrifying. Especially with the darkness hunting for her just beyond the flowering walls.

As if on cue, Nixie and Beck melted away into the kitchen as Marigold stroked back the princess' hair again with a motherly hand. She was entirely too forward, too familiar, and yet none of those boundaries seemed to exist in the cottage. Quite the contrary, Katerina found herself leaning into the hand in spite of herself, closing her eyes and savoring every touch.

"I know it's frightening, my dear, but rest assured, no harm will come to you as long as you are in this house. You can sleep easy for the night. We'll figure out what to do in the morning."

The little cup seemed to hum with anticipation, and after one last moment of deliberation the princess threw caution to the wind and swallowed it all in one gulp. In an instant, a feeling of overwhelming drowsiness came over her. Her eyelids started to droop before she'd even set down the mug, and the others were quick to rearrange the cushions as she leaned back onto the couch.

"Thank you..." she murmured, succumbing quickly to the tea's power and the night's fatigue. "All of you. I don't...I don't know what I would have done..."

Her voice trailed off as her eyes fluttered shut. Her crimson hair spilled out over the pillow, and for the first time since she entered the house a look of almost childlike tranquility settled over her lovely face.

The fairies stared for a long moment before Marigold tucked a blanket around her shoulders and waved the others away. They would let her sleep. No doubt, whatever happened tomorrow was going to be just as trying as whatever had happened last night. She might be safe for now, but the three of them couldn't keep away the shadows that chased her forever.

The poor girl was going to need all the sleep she could get...

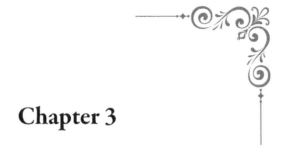

Chapter 3

KATERINA SLEPT THE rest of the day, the rest of the night, and late into the next morning. By the time she finally opened her eyes, stretching sleepily, she had all but forgotten where she was.

"Madge," she called, lowering her feet to the floor, "could you bring me some—"

She fell off the sofa with a little shriek, landing on the floor in an undignified heap. An inexplicable cloud of pink dust rose up beneath her, and she sneezed loudly, remembering for the first time that she had left the castle far behind.

"Well, look who finally woke up!"

Before she could even push to her feet, Nixie pranced into the house with an armful of flowers. She flashed the princess a quick smile before curling her fingers through the air in a strange cutting sort of gesture. A glass vase appeared from nowhere, rattling on the kitchen counter as the fairy dropped the flowers inside and hurried back to the living room, perching lightly upon the armrest of the sofa as she stared down at her guest.

"What are you doing on the floor?"

Katerina stared up into the fairy's enormous, curious eyes, and before she knew it she found herself smiling as well. She didn't understand what her father had meant when he'd told her that all magical creatures were dangerous and not to be trusted. If anything, the young fairy reminded her of girls she'd grown up with at the castle. Spirited, sweet, and entirely too curious for her own good.

"I was checking for mice," she teased. "So far so good."

The little fairy erupted into yet another fit of laughter, swelling the blossoms in the vase as she rocked back and forth, clinging onto the sides of the sofa for balance. Her vibrant hair danced in the air around her, then floated up in a little cloud as she hopped down to help Katerina to her feet.

"You know," she chirped, tugging the princess into the kitchen where a plate of biscuits and milk had been set out on the table, "you're nothing like what I imagined a princess would be. To start, you seem to have forgotten your crown."

Katerina grinned as she sat down at the table, realizing with the first bite that she'd never been so hungry in her entire life. "The queen gets a crown; the princess only gets a tiara."

"A *tiara*," Nixie repeated breathlessly, trying out the word for the first time. Her eyes drifted away as she tried to imagine it before darkening with a sudden frown. "Well, then, shouldn't you be getting a crown? Since the king died and everything?"

The princess froze with a biscuit halfway to her mouth as the little fairy clapped a hand over her mouth, as if she could drag the words back inside. Her enormous eyes swelled to an even greater size before she pushed forward with the most awkward conversational segue ever.

"...you want honey with that?"

Katerina stared at her in shock, completely blown away by the fairy's complete lack of filter, and she felt herself warming with another inexplicable smile. "Honey would be great."

As Nixie danced off to the cupboards to get some, she took a tiny sip of milk—feeling her strength start to return to her, bite by bite. As she chewed, she tried very hard to put things into perspective. Yes, she should be in the throne room right now, kneeling on the velvet carpet as the priest placed the crown upon her head. No, she shouldn't be sitting in a woodland cottage, accepting honey from a winged girl who came up to her waistline.

But you don't get to choose your stars, and she was making the best of the hand that was dealt to her. For now, she was alive. For now, that would have to do.

"You know," she said through a mouthful of biscuit, "you're nothing like how I imagined a fairy would be either."

Nixie leaned forward across the table, her eyes wide with anticipation.

"Better or worse?"

Katerina laughed. "Better—much better. Just...different." She took another bite, dousing the feathery pastry in a spoonful of honey. "To start, I didn't think you'd be able to talk."

Nixie's little face screwed up in disbelief.

"Not able to talk?! How could people even think—"

The door pushed open and Marigold and Beck swept inside, seemingly oblivious to the handfuls of leaves and twigs that had accumulated in their hair.

"I, for one, think it might be quite a relief," Marigold said innocently, "if *some* of us were temporarily relived of that particular ability..."

Katerina pursed her lips to hide a smile, but Nixie was confused. She stared between them all for a moment before her face lit with sudden understanding.

"Oh," she dropped her voice to a conspiratorial whisper, "do you mean Beck?"

Before the other fairy's inevitable retaliation, Marigold sent them both outside. Ordering them to *flower the garden*—whatever that meant—so she could speak to the princess in peace.

"I must apologize," she said with a sigh as the door swung shut behind them. "We don't get visitors from foreign parts very often. I'm afraid they're a little overexcited."

Judging by the explosion of multi-colored sparks shooting up from the garden, 'overexcited' was putting it mildly.

"They're wonderful," Katerina said earnestly. "You all are. I mean it. You've all been so kind...I don't really know how to repay you."

The fairy shook her head dismissively, her golden curls swishing back and forth. "It was our pleasure, Your Highness. There's no payment necessary. Except..." A very peculiar expression flitted across her face as she looked the princess up and down. "...except to remember. Remember what you've seen here. Remember the kindness you were shown."

Katerina set down her glass of milk, staring curiously at the little woman. "Well, of course I will. I don't know how I could ever forget."

The fairy brightened with a beaming smile.

"In that case, it's time we sent you on your way. It's already coming up on midday, and we'll have to get a move on if we want to make it to the village before dusk."

"Sent me on my way?" Katerina straightened up in alarm, shaken by the sudden change in conversation. "I'd hoped...I'd hoped maybe I could stay here for a few days. At least until I came up with some kind of plan—"

"My dear, I wish you could. But you're hardly five leagues outside the castle lands. The last thing you should do is linger so close. No, we must get you as far away as we can."

"But this place is protected," Katerina argued, her voice rising in panic. "I saw it myself. It doesn't look like anything to the outside world, until you work your magic on it."

A strange emotion swept across Marigold's face. An emotion that made the sun itself seem to dim as she reached across the table and took the princess' hand with a sad smile.

"You really know nothing of this world, do you?" she murmured thoughtfully, more to herself than to Katerina. "You're innocent to all this."

Katerina's mouth fell open in surprise, but she could think of nothing to say. It certainly hadn't been the answer she had been expecting, and yet she felt as though all three fairies had been thinking the same thing about her since the moment she arrived.

"There are different kinds of magic," the fairy continued kindly. "Our magic comes from the light. It's meant only to make things brighter, do you understand? It wouldn't do anything to shield you from the darkness that is sure to come."

The princess' heart fell as she glumly stared out the window. Come to think of it, she couldn't see either Beck or Nixie putting up much of a fight against assassins.

"No," Marigold continued thoughtfully, "you need to be with someone who can keep you safe. Someone who can protect you. Someone who's done this sort of thing before..."

For a second, all was quiet. Then it was like a light clicked on. Marigold's eyes lit up with sudden inspiration before settling upon Katerina, twinkling with a knowing smile.

"And I know just the man..."

THE TRIP DOWN TO THE village took the rest of the day, and considering that Katerina had recently trekked over miles of mountains in the dark, by the time they saw the thatched roofs and stone chimneys of the town square she was dead on her feet.

"Is that it?" she panted as the four of them came to a stop on a nearby hill. "Please tell me that's it. If it isn't, I vote that we give up and set up camp right here—"

"That's it," Marigold chuckled, staring down at the twinkling lights of the little village. "And the last thing you're going to want to do is spend another night sleeping out in the cold."

Fair point.

Katerina wrapped her travelling cloak tighter around her and began walking down the grassy incline, until she suddenly realized that the fairies were no longer behind her. In a fright, she turned around to see that they were all standing exactly where they'd stopped at the top of the hill.

"What's the matter? Aren't you coming?"

Marigold shook her head, and the others flashed her apologetic smiles.

"I'm afraid not, my dear. Our kind never goes into the village. Not unless we have to." She tilted her head sagely, as if she was quoting a parable. "Spend too much time in the company of humans, and there's no telling what nonsense might rub off on you."

Nixie and Beck made a strange movement, almost as if they were crossing themselves, and Katerina fought the impulse to roll her eyes.

Spend too much time in the company of fairies, and it's likely to turn your hair blue.

"I'll try not to take offense at that." She glanced quickly over her shoulder, ears perking up at the distant clamor of the town, a feeling of dread stealing into her chest. "At any rate, can't you at least walk me down to the village? I don't...I don't want to be alone."

She felt stupid saying it. Like a child who burst into their parents' room, only to flush and mumble something about having a bad dream. Still, with memories of her brother's hell hounds still fresh in her mind, it was impossible to hold back the question.

A look of genuine sympathy stared back at her from three affectionate faces, but for the second time Marigold shook her head.

"My dear, this is where we must part ways. But fear not, you will soon be in safe hands."

Katerina suppressed a sigh, staring down at a folded piece of paper between her fingers.

"You mean with this... Dylan Aires?"

How could they just send her off with someone she didn't know? With someone whose whereabouts they didn't know? They simply said the best place to start looking was at the local bar.

Nixie and Beck exchanged a quick look, while Marigold gestured almost sternly to the paper in her hand. "You be sure to give that to him. No matter what, make sure he reads it."

My entire life depends on whether a drunken stranger reads a fairy's secret note. Typical.

"I will." Katerina folded the note and tucked it into her cloak. "And I really can't tell you enough how grateful I am for your help. All of you." Her eyes swept over each one in turn, misting over with an emotion she couldn't control. "It's a kindness I'll not soon forget. I promise."

Nixie and Beck lit up with matching grins, while Marigold took a step forward. Despite their comical height difference she put her hand on the princess' shoulders, staring deep in her eyes.

"I may not know what the next chapter has in store, but I do know this: There is no such thing as chance, Katerina. You were brought here for a reason. All you must do now is have the strength and patience to find out what that reason might be."

...and find a way to stay alive in the meantime.

Her fear must have shown in her eyes, because Marigold gave her an extra squeeze.

"Just find Dylan Aires. He'll keep you safe." She took a step back as the others clustered around her on the top of the hill. "The rest is up to you."

A sudden bout of drunken laughter echoed up from the canyon below, followed by a shower of sparks as a flagon of ale tumbled carelessly into the roaring bonfire. Katerina's eyes widened as she glanced over her shoulder, staring into the flames, before a sudden panic took hold.

"But Marigold," she gasped, whirling back around, "what if I can't—"

It was too late. The fairies were already gone.

"—find him."

Like a deflating balloon, Katerina felt all the hope, and warmth, and security the three little creatures brought with them fade away in the chilly breeze. One second, she had been in a party of four. Protected by magic. Fortified with biscuits. And just like that she was on her own again. Just a lost traveler standing alone in the middle of the night... hoping to find her way in from the cold.

She stared once more at where the fairies had been standing, searching the hill uselessly for even the tiniest lingering glow, before turning slowly back to the village.

By now the sun had slipped completely below the horizon, and the place was coming alive at night. The roaring bonfire was the least of it. One by one, the shops were closing and the taverns were opening their doors. Scores of people—mostly men—were pouring out into the streets. Calling out loudly to one another. Shaking off the hard day's work before heading inside to drink it off for good measure. Hunters were making their way back from the nearby woods with their daily kills, to sell the next day at market. Teams of soot-covered workers were coming back in from the mine. Farmers, burned and beaten by the sun, were finally putting their heavy gloves aside to join the rest of them as they celebrated the end of another long week.

Life had been hard for the villages since the rebellion. Katerina was ashamed to say that her father didn't help. His idea of subduing his subjects was taxing them into oblivion. A policy that had accrued no small amount of resentment from the people whose backs were breaking under its weight. Anti-monarchy sentiment was high, and the more she thought about it the more Katerina suddenly understood the real reason for the bonfire. The real reason spirits were so high.

The king is dead. His people are celebrating.

A wave of fear swept over her as she nervously tucked her red hair into her cloak.

...and his daughter is coming to stay.

She was almost on the verge of turning around. She was almost on the verge of forgetting this Dylan Aires altogether and setting out on her own. But Marigold was right. She might also have been hopelessly unrealistic, but she was right. If Katerina stood even a chance at making it to see the next full moon, she needed protection. And in order to get that protection, she needed to go into that town.

"Come on, you little coward, one foot in front of the other..."

DESPITE HER PRESENT state of hysteria, Katerina made the greatest possible effort to compartmentalize those feelings as she marched down the hill and onto the dusty streets of the village. A hundred different dialects, and smells, and strange creatures bustled around in the night beside her, but she kept her face a perfect mask of calm, eyes locked on the road.

Marigold had been right about something else as well: She *was* innocent to the ways of the world. And if she wasn't careful, that innocence was going to get her killed.

"Watch your step!"

She gasped, and leapt out of the way as a wagon full of empty milk bottles went careening past her. The driver turned around long enough to make a very rude hand gesture before turning back to the road, on a race to get to the next village before dawn.

Her heart pounded as she stared down at the giant ruts in the mud—just inches away from where she had been standing just a moment before. Had no one else seen what had happened? The villagers were carrying on exactly as before. Did no one else think it was at all strange that a man almost killed a young woman and then screamed at her in the middle of the street?

Apparently not.

After another quick glance around, Katerina decided to take quick action. The longer she was on the street, the more she risked being recognized. She needed to find the tavern the fairies had told her about as fast as possible. Before any other milk wagons went careening her way.

"Excuse me?" She tugged on the sleeve of the safest-looking pedestrian, safe being on a relative sort of scale. At any rate, it was one of the few women. "Have you heard of a place called The Dancing Bear? Do you know where I might find it?"

"The Dancing Bear?" the woman repeated in an accent thick as mud. She looked the princess up and down, not even bothering to hide her judgement. "And why in the world would a young thing like you want to go to The Dancing Bear? Interested in a new line of work?"

Katerina sensed there was something not quite appropriate in what the woman was implying, but she lowered her head politely and gave nothing away. "I'm meeting a friend."

The woman stared at her a second more, cocking her head down the street. "It's at the end of the block. Right before you get to the butcher. But I'd be careful if I was you." She reached out and touched the edge of Katerina's cloak, smoothing the fine material between her fingers. "All sorts go to The Bear. But I promise, there's not a soul there who looks like you."

Katerina's pulse quickened as she discreetly tugged herself away before the woman could get a better grip. "Thanks, I'll...I'll keep that in mind."

Without a backwards glance, she hurried away. Keeping her head low, and her fiery hair swept carefully out of sight, she headed down the street to the bar.

What kind of place had the fairies sent her to? Did they know about its reputation? And what kind of man could this Dylan Aires be if he made a habit of frequenting such a tavern?

Katerina had the sinking feeling she was about to find out.

Just a few minutes later, she slowed down as the bright lights of the tavern twinkled into view. It looked rather picturesque and peaceful from the outside, but already she could hear the sound of half a dozen drunken brawls going on inside. She froze a moment on the frosted sidewalk, silently debating the risk versus reward, before she decided to put her trust once again in the fairies, took a deep breath, and pushed open the heavy oak door.

It was everything she could have imagined... and so much worse.

Her eyes took a second to adjust to the dim light, then widened to little saucers as she stared out over the extraordinary scene. It was as if the entire magical community had come together under some sort of uneasy truce, and had then proceeded to drink their weight in alcohol.

There were creatures there that Katerina had never seen before. Creatures she only vaguely remembered from the captions and pictures of her childhood books. Men were laughing with shifters. Goblins were gambling with dwarves. A contingent of brightly-colored pixies was perched on a lantern hung by the stairwell, drinking from little thimbles of nectar, while a massive creature that looked suspiciously like a troll was dancing by himself in the corner.

The noise was deafening. The patrons seemed constantly on the verge of breaking into a fight. It was chaos. Absolute chaos. But no one seemed to mind in the slightest.

In fact, no one seemed to even notice.

Katerina ducked down with a gasp as a bottle of what she hoped was red wine shattered over her head. She was able to dodge the majority of it, and hurried quickly towards the bar, keeping her eyes on the floor and her hands pinned tightly to her sides.

Under any other circumstance, her entrance into such a place would have caused quite a commotion indeed. But the room was in such an uproar that people hardly noticed she'd passed by until she was safely on the other side of the table, her long cloak swishing quickly across the floor.

"What can I get for you?"

The question was fired out almost as soon as Katerina touched the counter. She'd expected the bartender to be the world's burliest man—the sort of person who could serve as an enforcer should the rowdy crowd get out of hand—but what turned around was one of the most beautiful women Katerina had ever seen. Her eyes widened for a moment as her lips parted in shock.

Never before had she seen such a blatant display of sexuality. Red lips, painted eyelids, and a deliberately torn dress that left very little to the imagination.

"Honey, you want a drink?"

On second thought, she didn't know if she'd call the woman beautiful. She was certainly striking, that much was sure. But there was something almost aggressive about the way she presented herself. Something that made the hairs on the back of Katerina's neck stand on end.

She quickly shook herself out of her trance and flashed a polite smile. "No, actually. I was hoping to book a room for the night. Is there a chance I could speak to the owner?"

The woman leaned back, her eyes sparkling with curiosity as she looked the new customer up and down. While she might have been able to hide her fiery hair, Katerina was completely unaware of the other rather obvious differences that set her miles apart.

"Bill!" the woman called over her shoulder, keeping the princess locked in her gaze all the while. "There's a girl here who wants a room. Doesn't look the type to rent by the hour..."

There was a tittering of laughter from those who were seated close to them at the bar, but before the flush had even died from Katerina's cheeks a tall grey-haired man hurried out from a room in the back, wiping his hands busily on his apron as he pulled out a worn ledger.

"A single room, you said?" He hardly even glanced up as he hastened to put on his spectacles. "Just for the night?"

"Yes, I believe so." Katerina leaned a bit closer, lowering her voice in an attempt for at least a mild degree of privacy. "I'm actually here looking for someone. A man named Dylan Aires." She paused hesitantly, staring hopefully across the bar. "Is there any chance you know who that is?"

It was a gamble, saying the name out loud. But by that point, Katerina didn't know what else she could do. Was she supposed to go around table by table? Canvass the entire bar?

"Dylan Aires, huh?" The curvaceous bartender started cleaning out an empty glass with a grin. "And what could a girl like you want with Dylan Aires?"

"Get back to work, Mika." The proprietor finished scribbling down in his ledger, then looked up at Katerina for the first time. His eyes did the slightest double-take before he raised his voice, somehow making it heard over the entire bar. "This young woman is looking for a Dylan Aires." He paused deliberately, eyes sweeping the room. "Is there anyone here by that name?"

There was a sudden hush as the bar abruptly fell quiet. People froze with cards still in hand, with drinks halfway to their mouths. Even the troll in the corner stopped dancing long enough to turn around with the others and look towards the bar.

A second later, all those eyes landed upon Katerina.

Oh...shit. Shit. Shit. Shit.

She tried her best to keep steady. Tried her best to meet the horde of probing eyes. It wasn't easy. From the second the man called out the name the entire place had frozen into the world's strangest assortment of statues.

The shifters were looking at her appraisingly, the dwarves were surveying the price of her fancy cloak, a young man in the corner was staring intently over the rim of his glass. And even as she stood there, four pale men with a table full of empty glasses pushed to their feet.

"How about it, folks?" the owner called out again. He was simply teasing her now, already preoccupied with the stack of papers in his hand. "Going once... going twice..."

"I can be your Dylan Aires."

Katerina's eyes shot up in surprise to land on a drunken man standing in the middle of the bar. He was holding a flagon of ale in the air—toasting the very idea—while all around him the icy tension in the room began to thaw and crack.

People relaxed. People started openly laughing. People started calling out, one by one.

"No, let me be your Dylan."

"No one could make a better Dylan than me."

"I'm the real Dylan. Come here, sweetheart, let me prove it to you..."

Katerina's heart fell as the bar slowly came back to life. A few moments and several obscene propositions later, the patrons had all but forgotten about the interruption. Only a few eyes lingered on her curiously, but she was quick to turn back to the bar. It was obvious these people didn't exactly like outsiders. Even if the outsider happened to be a young woman, travelling by herself. If the real Dylan Aires was anywhere in the vicinity he'd no doubt already heard about the commotion down at the tavern, and would be keeping his distance. Marigold's brilliant plan had failed.

Her fingers closed around the note in her pocket as her shoulders fell with a quiet sigh.

I might as well read it now. Since he'll never be reading it himself.

She was right about to pull it out and open it, when a cold hand tapped lightly upon her shoulder. Her head snapped up and she turned around in surprise, only to see the four pale men she'd noticed earlier—the ones who'd been sitting around a table full of empty glasses.

"Excuse me, miss?"

Up close, they were even paler than she'd realized. And far more beautiful. Snowy white skin offset with sparkling dark eyes. They each looked somewhat alike, close enough to be brothers, yet there was something entirely different about all four of them. And something not entirely safe.

"Yes?" Katerina pulled her cloak tighter around her, careful to keep her famous crimson hair out of view. She didn't know if news that the princess was on the run had left the castle, but if it had no young woman travelling alone would be above suspicion. Least of all, someone who looked like her. "Can I help you with something?"

"Quite the contrary." The man flashed a row of pearly white teeth. "I was rather hoping instead to buy you a drink. Forgive my impertinence, but you seem to be here on your own."

There was something strange about the way he said it. It was stranger still that his three friends remained silent behind him. And yet, Katerina felt herself drawn to the manner in which he spoke. Growing up in the castle, one learned to speak with a constant degree of formality. A degree that had been distinctly lacking on her journey thus far. It was nice to come across someone with manners. Especially when those manners were directed at her.

"I am," she said gratefully, "and thank you very much. But I'm afraid I'm going to have to decline. It's been a long day, and I'd really better get up to my room."

The man nodded curtly, but didn't move. Neither did his friends.

"A drink for me, then?"

Katerina glanced quickly between them, growing more confused all the while.

"I beg your pardon?"

The man's dark eyes glittered with a cool smile as he leaned closer, close enough that she could see the flames of a nearby lantern flickering across his pale face.

"Just a taste—you'll return to your room unharmed." His lips curved up in a chilling smile as he made to sweep back the hood of her cloak. "You must admit, you look most inviting..."

Katerina cringed from his touch, her eyes wide with fright, but a second before the man could touch her a figure blurred in between them, knocking his hand out of the air.

"I believe the lady said no."

The princess and the four strangers whirled around in identical surprise, gawking at the stranger in their midst. It was like he'd come out of nowhere, materializing from somewhere in the shadows. His back was towards her, so she couldn't see his face, but the other men could. And they clearly didn't like what they saw.

"Is that right?" The man who'd been reaching towards her took an instinctive step back, but was far from backing down entirely. Quite the contrary. With his three friends at his back, he seemed frightfully confident of his chances. "I heard nothing of the sort."

The man leaned against the counter, a picture of ease. Not only did the four-to-one odds not seem to faze him in the slightest, but Katerina could have sworn she saw the hint of a smile.

"Didn't you?" he asked innocently. "It must have been too quiet, as she seems unbearably polite. I believe what she meant to say was, *back the fuck off.*"

For a split second, all pretenses dropped. For a split second, Katerina saw a glimpse of what was about to come. Then the man flashed a bright smile.

"Or something along those lines..."

There was a strange hissing sound as the four friends gathered together. Gone was the pleasant demeanor. Gone were the charming smiles. As the façade finally cracked, Katerina was able to see them for what they really were. Not beautiful—enticing. Not polite—conniving.

A little shiver whispered up her spine as she took a step back, feeling as though she'd dodged a threat she hadn't even seen coming. If only for now. As grateful as she was for his presence, for the life of her she didn't see what chance the man possibly had. Not against four others.

"This hardly seems like a fair fight." The man who'd propositioned her stepped forward with an oily smile, looking his opponent up and down. "And I don't know if we'll be able to control ourselves once so much of your blood has spilled upon the floor."

Katerina paled with both fear and confusion, but the man protecting her simply smiled.

"Guess I'll have to take my chances then."

For a split second, nobody moved. Then, all at once, the bar was a blur of action.

The princess staggered back with a stifled shriek, clapping her hands over her mouth as she tried to reconcile the impossible scene. One second, her fearless protector had been standing in front of her. The next, he was some sort of mythological warrior come to life. Dazzling her eyes with the blinding grace with which he moved. Sending devastating vibrations up through the floorboards as he felled his opponents, one by one.

The first fool to step forward had his head smashed through the bar. The second was used as an unfortunate weapon to take out the third. And the last man? The man who'd come up to her and started all the trouble to begin with? He received the fiercest treatment of all.

A piercing cry echoed through the tavern as the man broke a glass and held the shards to her attacker's neck. Katerina watched in horror as the serrated edge trailed across his pale skin, leaving a fine line of crimson in the white. The rest of the patrons went perfectly still, and she was about to look away entirely, when the man suddenly dropped the glass, pointing to the door instead.

"I agree," he said quietly. "It wasn't a fair fight."

For a split second, it looked like the broken man wasn't going to accept the offer, that his pride would demand he cry to continue the fight. Then one of his companions groaned weakly by his feet, and he whirled around with an angry hiss—sweeping towards the door.

"We won't forget this," he swore as the four of them staggered out into the cold. "Not as long as we walk this earth—we will *never* forget this."

Katerina froze in terror, but her charming savior merely smiled—chuckling quietly as he reached across the bar and poured himself a shot of whiskey. "You know where to find me."

Bold words. Ones that sufficiently ended the conversation.

Just a second later, the door slammed shut.

A rush of blood poured back into Katerina's frozen limbs, and she felt as though she could breathe for the first time. Her eyes flickered anxiously to the back of the man's head, along with the rest of the bar, but he stayed right where he was—quietly sipping his whiskey. A few seconds later, his eyes drifted apologetically up to the owner, who looked back at him with a mixture of intense amusement and frustration. The barmaid joined in with a little grin before her boss leapt up onto the counter, stretching his arms out with a wide smile.

"Why so quiet? This isn't a house of prayer! The next round's on the house!"

The little tavern burst to life again as the fight was forgotten and people started pouring forward to get their free drinks. The man melted back into the crowd, leaving his own glass on the counter, and Katerina was quick to follow, desperate not to lose him in the crowd. She hurried this way and that, wishing desperately that she'd gotten a better look at his face, when a hand came out of nowhere and pulled her gently away from the drunken crowd.

"You were looking for Dylan Aires?"

Katerina stared up in disbelief, only to see a pair of blue eyes twinkling down at her.

"You just found him."

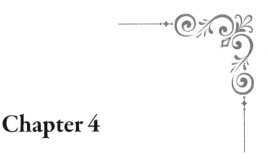

Chapter 4

TALK ABOUT BEING PUT on the spot. Considering all the hype and anticipation, now that Katerina was faced with Dylan head on she found herself at a complete loss as to what to say.

To be fair, there was no telling whether she would've been able to speak anyway. In her entire life—through all the royal gatherings and banquets, all the foreign dignitaries and eighteen years of processions—she had never met anyone quite like Dylan.

It was impossible to take your eyes off him.

Despite being dressed like a commoner, there was a strange kind of magnetism to him. The way he looked. The way he moved. Even in stillness, it was impossible to ignore. When he raised his eyes to look at something, other people turned around to see, too. When his lips twitched up in a smile, one felt compelled to discover the reason why—if only to prolong the experience. When he fixed those mesmerizing eyes on Katerina, she felt as though she'd been frozen still.

He had dark hair that swept across his face with an effortless sort of grace, and what her father would only describe as 'well-bred' features. High cheekbones, a strong jaw. There was a masculine sort of ruggedness about him, but an undeniable beauty as well. A beauty that stood out just as much in this filthy bar as did her own. A beauty he seemed determined to ignore himself.

When she simply stood there, at a loss for words, he cocked his head to the side, staring down at her as though there might be something broken in her head.

"...Good talking with you."

Without another word, he turned on his heel and started walking away.

It wasn't until he'd gone back to the bar that Katerina's senses returned to her and she came back to life. "Wait!" She battled her way through the crowd and slid onto the stool next to him, grabbing hold of his sleeve. A pointed look made her carefully retract her hand, but she had no intention of letting him go a second time. "I'm sorry, I didn't mean to stare. It's just...*you're* Dylan?"

Looks aside, she had expected someone much, much older. The strong, silent, overly-bearded type. Preferably with a battle-ax permanently affixed to his hand.

Dylan didn't speak again, as he'd already answered the question. He simply inclined his head and stared down at her, waiting for an explanation.

An explanation she was still too shell-shocked to give.

"You...you saved my life." She wasn't quite sure how she knew, but she was suddenly certain that those men had no intention of letting her walk away. That, instead, they had every intention of killing her.

He snapped his fingers for another whiskey, laying a bronze coin upon the bar. "It seemed like someone should."

Katerina blinked, completely stunned by his indifference. But something in her pressed on. "...and you're bleeding."

He glanced down at her for a moment before wiping a smudge off his forehead, looking highly inconvenienced by the whole thing. "You have a brilliant knack for stating the obvious."

Was he serious?! How was he being so...so casual about everything?!

She pulled her chair an inch or so closer, hoping that the random men leering at her around the bar would take it as a sign, even though the man in question was far more interested in his drink.

"I saw you sitting in the corner when the proprietor called out your name." She stared at him with wide eyes, trying desperately to latch on to anything she could. "You didn't come forward."

Not only that, but he was clearly *never* going to come forward. He'd glanced up just long enough to see what was going on before returning to his drink—smiling to himself as various creatures started piping up around the bar, claiming to be him.

"I didn't answer because I didn't want to speak to you."

What?

She flinched, stung by the blunt honesty. Never in her life had someone dared speak to her that way. Let alone a stranger who was miles beneath her rank. Let alone when she was already on the verge of tears. He saw her reaction and softened a fraction of a degree.

"In these parts, it isn't exactly wise to answer an open call. You never know who might be looking for you, or why." A flicker of curiosity danced through his eyes as he made a quick study of her face. "I only say that because you're clearly not from around these parts." He finished his whiskey and set down the glass, turning to face her. The chit-chat part of the conversation had clearly come to an end. He wanted answers now. "Who are you? Why did you ask for me?"

Moment of truth. Katerina's hands curled around the note in her pocket. Did she give it to him right now, in the middle of the busy tavern? And how much exactly was he allowed to know?

The fairies obviously thought he could be trusted, but he only looked a year or two older than Katerina was herself. And, yes, he had technically just saved her life but, to be honest, it seemed like more of an afterthought. Something he merely did on the way to get his drink.

"Well, you see..." She tucked her hair nervously into her cloak, feeling his smoldering eyes burning into her skin. "I mean, the thing is..."

A flagon of ale crashed down on the counter between them, putting an end to her quiet explanation before it could even get off the ground. But the flagon was the least of her troubles.

"Well, well, well! Look who suddenly remembered his own name!"

Dylan and Katerina turned at the same time as Mika, the beguiling barmaid, set down her towel and joined the conversation, positioning herself firmly between the two.

"So, I see you found him." She winked at Katerina before leaning all the way over the bar, giving Dylan a clear view of her bosom as she flashed him a seductive smile. "And here we were, all prepared to keep your secret till the bitter end."

Katerina stiffened uncomfortably, discreetly looking away while Dylan chuckled softly.

"Never really thought loyalty was one of your strong suits."

Mika flashed another smile, pleased with his teasing. "Maybe not, but I have other talents."

His lips twitched up in a caustic grin. "So I've heard."

Katerina blinked in shock, unable to believe she was hearing what she was hearing. At the castle, people were only as forward as three centuries of etiquette and a corset would allow, but Mika was on a roll. She leaned down even further, casually reaching for his hand.

"I'd love to show you sometime."

He shifted just as casually away, thoroughly unfazed by her advances. "Sometime. Right now, I'd just like to see you pour."

The back and forth came to a sudden stop. A second later Mika straightened up, staring across the counter in confusion. "Excuse me?"

"Whiskey. Two of them," he added with a nod to Katerina, placing another bronze coin upon the counter. "You drink, don't you, princess?"

Katerina's face went pale as her eyes flashed up in terror. "...why would you call me that?"

A peculiar smile flitted across Dylan's face, while Mika merely rolled her eyes and poured two glasses of the thick, amber liquid. The smell of it saturated the air, burning the inside of the princess' nose as she forced the awkward moment behind them, and held it up for a tentative sniff.

Holy hells! How can anyone drink this stuff?!

Her revulsion must have showed on her face, because Dylan chuckled again as Mika shook her head, looking distinctly unimpressed. "*This* is why you're blowing me off? For *her?*"

"Don't be unkind." His eyes danced with amusement as they rested upon the princess. "I'm sure she has a few hidden talents herself."

Mika scoffed as if this was highly unlikely, while Katerina blushed to the roots of her hair. In a desperate attempt to fit in she took a brave gulp of whiskey, fighting back a gasp of shock as her eyes watered involuntarily. It was like swallowing liquid fire. A far cry from the floral wines and sparkling ales of the castle. Whatever was in that cup would be better used resuscitating the dead.

"It's..." she cleared her throat and forced a pained smile, "it's very good."

Dylan's eyes twinkled as he took a sip from his own glass, but Mika's rather limited patience had reached an end. She was unwilling to admit defeat. And she was just as unwilling to let her prize go off with someone she deemed highly unworthy.

"Seriously, how many times are you going to keep saying no to me?" She ignored Katerina completely, plumping her lips out in a sexy pout. "I've got a room upstairs. You know you want to." This time she caught his hand, lacing her long fingers through his own.

For a split second, a strange, vacant expression came over his face before he tugged his wrist away with a rueful grin. "What I *want* is to live to see tomorrow morning."

She stepped back with a playful smile. "Call it a lack of imagination on your part."

"More like a vested interest in my own self-preservation."

With a parting grin he pushed to his feet, holding out an arm and gesturing for Katerina to do the same. She quickly followed after him, completely baffled by what had just happened.

"You never know." Mika cast him a wistful look as the two of them melted away into the crowd, picking up her towel and returning to the glasses. "You might get lucky..."

For whatever reason, the words gave Katerina chills as she followed her unlikely savoir to the same private booth he'd already claimed in the back. It wasn't until she sat down that she realized the strategic advantage of such a position. He was back far enough to have a view of the entire tavern, and close enough to the exit to make a quick getaway if he so desired.

Katerina's eyes were still lingering on the door, when he cleared his throat quietly, summoning her attention.

"As you were saying—"

"What did you mean?" Katerina interrupted with wide eyes. "That you wanted to live to see tomorrow morning?"

Dylan paused, a little taken aback, before his eyes flickered reflexively to the bar. "Mika's a succubus. It would be an amazing night, but it would also be my last."

Well, that explains it!

While the succubae were a little too racy for her royal nursery books, Katerina had heard some of the male servants talking about them. Supernatural temptresses who lured men to their deaths by enticing them to bed. They were supposed to be nearly impossible to resist. Even more so if they managed to lay a hand on your bare skin. She didn't know how Dylan managed to do it.

"But surely she can't want to kill you!"

Katerina had only observed them for a short time, but despite the dangerous banter there was a playfulness to the way they interacted. She'd even go so far as to say they were friends.

Dylan shrugged good-naturedly, as if these things could seldom be helped.

"It's what she is—you can hardly blame her. Just like you can hardly blame those vampires."

Oh yeah? Why don't you watch me blame...wait...what?!

Katerina froze perfectly still, a beautiful statue amidst the frenzy of the bar. "Did you say...vampires?"

Dylan took a swig of whiskey, staring at her over the rim of the glass. Unable to decide whether or not she was joking. In the end, he decided to take her at her word.

"What did you think they were—men? And honestly," he gestured to her with a careless wave of his hand, "what did you expect?"

"*Excuse* me?" Her eyebrows shot into her hair as she bristled defensively. "What the hell is that supposed to mean? I should *expect* to get attacked, just because I'm a woman on my own—"

"You're covered in blood."

Well, *that* stopped her in her tracks.

At first she just stared at him, convinced that she must have misheard. Then a couple of things started clicking into place. The glass that had broken over her head when she'd first walked through the door. The one she'd hoped was red wine. The way the four pale men had stood up the second they laid eyes on her, sniffing the air eagerly as they wound their way through the crowd.

A drink for me, then, the vampire had said. *Just a taste.*

Katerina reached up to touch the damp hood of her cloak in horror.

Well, no wonder! It's like walking around with a giant 'EAT ME' sign around my neck!

"You could always take it off," Dylan said casually, gesturing to the slick fabric. "Unless you're going for the whole goth-chic look. In which case, you're taking it a bit too seriously."

Instead of taking his suggestion Katerina pulled the cloak tighter around herself, glaring at the beautiful man with growing dislike. "Is everything a damn joke to you—"

"Why were you looking for me?"

There was no preamble. No wind-up to give her any warning. People living on the outskirts of the kingdom had learned long ago to dispense with wasted words. They cut to the core of a matter. No pretenses. No delays. Just the cold, hard truth.

Still...she didn't know exactly what to say. It was no ordinary secret she was carrying. It was the kind of secret that could topple an empire. The kind of secret that could get her killed.

After a second of waiting, Dylan shifted impatiently. "All right, let's start with something easier. Why don't you tell me your name?"

Crap...not easier at all.

Katerina blanched, her mind racing as she simultaneously blanked on every single human name. When those didn't work, she decided to go with an inhuman one. "Marigold."

Dylan leaned back in surprise, his sky-blue eyes taking in every detail of her face. It was clearly not the answer he'd been expecting. "Your name is—"

"Marigold sent me to find you. She seemed to think that you could help me." Katerina fumbled quickly in her pocket, pulling out the note. "Here. She said to give you this."

He didn't reach for the note. He didn't even acknowledge it. It lay on the table between them. A silent invitation.

One he clearly had no intention of accepting.

"Marigold sent you to find me," he repeated slowly, testing out the words for truth. When Katerina only nodded his eyes narrowed slightly, fixing with unnerving intensity on her face. "Well, if you met Marigold, then I take it you met her sisters, Freya and Nair."

"Nixie and Beck?" the princess answered, rising to the challenge. "Yes, we've met."

He gave a slight nod, temporarily satisfied. But still, he had yet to even look at the note, and Katerina's skin had broken out in a cold sweat. Finally, after a full minute of silence, he took a swig of his drink, hardly blinking as the aged whiskey burned down his throat. "So why is Marigold under the impression that you need my help?" he asked bluntly. "I'm assuming you're in some kind of trouble."

An image of her brother's hell hounds flashed through her head, and Katerina stifled a shudder. Trouble? Yeah, you could say that. She almost felt guilty bringing it to his door. "The thing is, I've sort of...run away from home." She hesitated nervously, editing on the fly. "My family will have sent people after me, the kind of people who make those vampires look tame, but I can't go back. No matter what happens...I can't go back."

She'd tried to keep her voice as steady as possible. Tried to ignore the hell hounds, and the frightening tavern, and her blood-soaked clothing. She tried to tune it all out and simply force herself to keep pushing forward. But after everything that had happened...it was a lost cause.

A visible tremble shook her shoulders as the tiniest sigh escaped her lips. It was a sigh of pure exhaustion. As defeated as it was resigned.

Dylan didn't miss a thing.

His eyes swept over her with growing curiosity. Curiosity, and another emotion that was harder to identify. Was it sympathetic? Was it protective? For a split second he glanced down, and it looked as though he was going to pick up the note right then and there. But a stronger, more practiced, side of him held back. The side that had learned to keep his head down and mind his own business. The kind that had learned the hard way not to get tangled up in the troubles of strangers.

Instead, he stalled for time. Rehashing the facts. Getting the full sum of the story.

"So I take it you ran away from home straight into Marigold's arms? And you've been hiding out from these familial repercussions ever since?"

Katerina nodded quickly. It was obvious there were quite a few gaps in her tale, but if he was going to be gracious enough to overlook them she certainly wasn't going to press. "Yes, that's right."

There was a slight pause before he broke her gaze and looked down at the table.

"And she sent you to me?" A faint smile ghosted across his face before he drained what was left of his whiskey, muttering under his breath. "Interfering, self-important fairies..."

By now, Katerina was on the edge of her seat. Hardly daring to move. Hardly daring to breathe as she watched his every move. Waiting to see what he would do next. "So...does that mean that you'll—"

"Sorry, princess. Can't help."

In a brisk movement he was up from the table, leaving the whole dismal story behind him as he headed for the door. He'd left the note, too.

Katerina stared after him in shock. Unable to believe it was true. Unable to believe that the fairies could be so wrong. That their home-town hero was leaving her to fend for herself. It took a second for her to find her feet. For her to snatch up the note and race after him.

"Wait!" She pushed open the heavy door and ran out into the street. By now, the full moon had risen high above the little village and a gust of frigid air hit her right in the face, stunning her senseless. She squinted her eyes as she tried to find him in the dark.

It wasn't easy. Unlike the bright colors and opulent shades of the castle, everything here seemed to be in earth tones. Worn creams. Dirtied browns. Dark, weathered boots. It wasn't until he passed under the light of a distant store front that she saw him again striding purposefully into the night as the moon streaked silver into his dark hair.

She took after him without a second thought. Tearing down the middle of the road. Pushing past whatever scattered pedestrians were still left on the street. Hardly noticing anything going on around her, until she'd shoved him in the back as hard as she could.

"What the he—" He whirled around in surprise, but by that time she'd already recovered her balance. And her anger.

Her arms were folded tightly around her chest, and her eyes flashed pure fire as they burned into him in the dark. "So that's it?!" she demanded. "You're just walking away?!"

He blinked incredulously. "Did you just *push* me?"

She pushed him again. "Like it never even happened! Like we never even met!"

He stumbled backwards in surprise, staring down at her ineffectual hands. "What are you—six?"

"I will NOT make any apologies!" she shouted. "I am fighting for my LIFE!"

He stared at her in shock for a moment before recovering himself, smoothing down his disheveled clothes and raking his fingers through his hair. "And I wish you the best of luck with that. But it's not going to involve me."

He tried to turn again but she grabbed his arm, pulling with all her might. For a moment, he merely stared down at his sleeve, both astonished and exasperated at the same time. Then he seemed to take pity on her and reluctantly turned back. Either that, or he didn't want to rip his coat.

"So the fairies were wrong to trust you," she spat, channeling every bit of misdirected rage into a single moment, onto a single target. "You're not a savior, you're just a drunk."

He opened his mouth to answer, but seemed to think better of it. There was something too desperate about her to challenge. Something too despondent to engage. Instead, he merely agreed with a tip of his head. "That's me. Just a drunk. And I'd best be getting home."

She threw up her hands with a bitter laugh—all the fears and emotions of the last few days catching up as hysterical tears began pouring down her face. "Of course you should! Please, don't let my impending death keep you from any of the fascinating things I'm sure you had planned for the evening. Mucking out the stables, feeding the pigs…"

His eyes flashed as they glanced about the darkened street before he reached out suddenly and grabbed her arm. The tears stopped immediately as she stared up at him in terror. She knew this man could fight. She knew this man could kill. And here she was, yelling at him in the middle of the street, giving him every possible motivation to do exactly that.

"Three things."

While he was clearly just as incensed as she, he didn't raise his voice to make it known. He lowered it instead. Speaking in a dangerously soft clip.

"First of all, you don't know a thing about me or my life. So keep your delightful opinions to yourself. Second, no one in this world is under any obligation to help you. Do you understand? You chose to leave, that's it. You're on your own. Simple as that. Don't go around expecting a hand up, because that's just not the way things work around here."

He released her arm just as abruptly as he'd grabbed it, leaving her trembling and shaken in its wake. The reality of her situation was beginning to settle upon her but, strangely enough, she didn't blame him in the slightest. He was right—he was under no obligation. Nothing that had happened had anything to do with him, let alone was his fault. He was just a man whose name she'd heard from a trio of lunatic fairies. The nightmare? The men chasing after her in the night?

Those were hers to deal with alone.

"What's the third thing?"

He looked down in surprise at the sudden change of her tone. The lifeless sort of resignation that dulled her sharp words. It was as if a light had gone out. One that wouldn't rekindle.

"Excuse me?"

Her eyes glassed over as she stared blankly into the dark, hardly aware of what she was saying. "You said there were three things, but you only said two. What's the third?"

For the first time all night, the hint of an apology flashed across his handsome face. It was obviously a feeling he wasn't accustomed to, and it didn't linger long. But it was there for a moment.

"You might want to rinse off some of that blood. Can never be too careful in these parts."

Their eyes met for a fleeting moment before she took a step back. The roaring bonfire had simmered down to coals, and her time in the tiny village had come to an end. In the morning she'd be leaving, for better or worse. Her lips twitched up in a lifeless smile as she nodded in farewell. "Thanks for the tip."

Before he could open his mouth to respond, she was already walking away. Sparing not a glance behind her. Keeping her bloodshot eyes locked on the shadowy road. When she was about halfway back to the tavern, she rifled around in her pocket and tossed the note from the fairies onto the street. She wouldn't be needing it. Not anymore.

Just one night, then you'll leave this place behind. Just one night, then you'll start off someplace new.

Little did she know the night was just getting started...

Chapter 5

THE ROOM KATERINA BOOKED for the night looked like something she'd find in the servant's corridor back at the castle. A simple cot. A rickety dresser. And a thick taper sitting on the windowsill to allow for light. On second thought, it was more like a room she'd find in the stables.

Nevertheless, she locked the door quickly and sank down into the center of the sagging bed, glad to be away from prying eyes no matter the circumstances. Although she'd only left the fairies a few hours before, and had only left the castle a few days before that, she felt as though she'd been running for as long as she could remember. Running and looking over her shoulder. Terrified as to who might be running after her. Petrified as to who she might see.

With an exhausted sigh, she pulled off her cloak and settled down beneath the threadbare comforter, ignoring the pieces of straw that poked through the mattress. She quickly added the cloak as a secondary blanket, vowing to clean off the blood first thing in the morning.

Can never be too careful in these parts...

Dylan's words echoed back to her as she lay there in the dark, a chilling reminder that the real world was nothing like her childhood storybooks. That life had grown harder, and the people had hardened with it. There were no heroes or happily-ever-afters. Empathy, optimism, and the belief in miracles had long since died. The most people wanted now was to simply survive.

And she must become one of them.

With another shaky sigh, she blew out the candle and closed her eyes. Praying she wouldn't dream. Praying she would simply fall asleep.

But it wasn't meant to be.

CRASH!

Katerina's eyes shot open with a gasp as the wooden door to her room was kicked clean off the hinges. The blinding light of a dozen torches came pouring in, and before she could make sense of what was going on—before she could even identify her attackers—she was being lifted straight out of bed and dragged down the stairs. Her bare feet knocked painfully against the steep steps, and by the time she reached the ground floor she finally caught her breath enough to let out a scream.

But a single scream was all she got.

The second she cried out, she was struck over the head with something heavy enough to leave her in a daze. Her eyes fluttered open and shut, and her head dropped weakly to the side as she was carried out of the tavern and into the freezing night.

"What..." she murmured weakly, trying to stay awake. "What's going on—"

There was a sharp slap, and her world darkened once more. It didn't come back into focus until she was suddenly dropped onto the wet street. She lay in a daze, staring up at her attackers.

...not that she had to look up too far.

Dwarves?

She couldn't believe it. As the world blinked slowly back into focus, she found herself face to face with the same group of creatures she'd seen earlier in the tavern. The ones who were greedily eyeing her fancy travelling cloak. At the time, she'd been too preoccupied with far more immediate concerns to give them much thought. But now, it was easy to see that this was their plan all along.

Fortunately, they cared not for her. Only for her money.

"You'll speak when you're spoken to!" The same dwarf who had slapped her raised his hand in warning. He did it once, he'd do it again. "Until then—you'll keep quiet!"

"Yes, but we need her to speak," another dwarf grumbled under his breath, one hand fiddling nervously with his long beard. "To tell us about her relations."

There was an awkward beat of silence as everyone froze.

"Yes, I was just getting to that!" the first dwarf snapped defensively, glaring down at the fallen princess as if it was somehow all her fault. "You, girl, tell us about your family!"

My family?

Katerina went pale as ice, kneels curling into her chest as she stared up at the ring of little men circling her. They weren't much to look at from afar but she knew now that, despite their size, they possessed unnatural strength. And the fact that they were asking about her family—

How could they have possibly guessed? What could they possibly know?

"My...my family?" she stuttered, staring helplessly around the ring. She was on the verge of making a run for it but they had her completely surrounded, and she had the sneaking suspicion the little bastards were a lot faster than they looked. "What do you mean?"

"What do you *think* he means?" A dwarf with a giant ear-horn spat on the ground as the tiny fellow hovering near his elbow glanced nervously down the street. "Where do your people come from? How many of them are still alive? How are we to get in contact?"

Katerina flinched at from his tone, but she was still at a complete loss. Not only did she have no idea what they were trying to get at, but she was understandably a little distracted by the deadly collection of weapons the gang was wearing on their belts.

A man wielding what looked like a pick-ax was especially intimidating.

"I'm sorry...get in contact?" She looked from one to the next in a panic, trying desperately to understand. "Why would you want to—"

"Do you not get what this is, lady?!" The dwarf who'd spat on the ground before took an angry step forward, waving his little arms. "We intend to ransom you! Clothes like this means you obviously come from money, and since you're travelling alone I'm willing to bet that whoever lost you would be willing to pay a lot of money to get you back! Honestly, are you *stupid*?!"

He hit the side of his head so hard that the ear-horn popped right out.

The rest of the dwarves stared down at it, but said nothing. Katerina stared up at her abductors, but had no idea where to start. Should she just make up a family? Should she say that they'd all died? What province should she say they hailed from?

...shouldn't someone pick up that poor man's ear-horn?

"Actually," she began hesitantly, "I lost my family. Just a few weeks ago. My village supported me for as long as they could, and when that stopped I set out on my own."

A profound silence followed this remark. She couldn't tell whether it was a good or a bad thing. Resisting the urge to over-embellish with details, as was her custom, she lowered her eyes to the ground, praying for someone to venture onto the street and see her there.

Not that I should expect any help...

"You lost your family, eh?" The tallest of the dwarves stepped forward, a man with a ginger beard that trailed all the way down to the street. "And how did that conveniently ill-timed tragedy come about?"

Katerina was almost offended. If she really had lost her family, that would have been an incredibly insensitive thing to say. Then again, she supposed the whole 'kidnap with the intent to ransom' thing was insensitive enough.

"They died in a fire," she murmured in a low voice, hoping like hell the tears in her eyes would be misconstrued as grief. "It destroyed our entire farm. I was away at a friend's. By the time I got back in the morning, everything was gone."

The dwarf's eyes flashed knowingly as he took a step forward, leaving his ring of companions behind. Up close, it was even easier to see that dwarves were clearly built for the mining that had made them so famous in the time before the rebellion, that had made them so valuable to the crown. That is, until the crown felt threatened like it always did and decided to decimate their entire race. The little fellow might have been small, but he was nothing but pure muscle.

And right now, all of it was directed straight at Katerina.

"A fire," he repeated softly, staring deep into her eyes. "And it destroyed your entire farm."

She'd thought it was a good excuse at the time, but suddenly it couldn't sound less believable. Her face flushed as he came even closer, towering over her as she huddled on the street.

"Pray tell, good lady...where was this farm?"

Game over.

A sudden chill swept over the princess as she realized she was out of cards. Yes, she'd studied the different provinces as a child back at the castle, but she couldn't remember any of their names let alone which ones were cities versus agricultural centers.

What was worse, she suspected the ginger dwarf knew it all along.

"It was..." She cringed as his eyes flashed with rage. "It was near..."

There was a ghastly profanity as the dwarf raised his hand once more.

Katerina braced for the impact, but just before he could strike several things happened at once.

A streak of light flashed through the darkness. The dwarf fell backwards with a gasp of surprise. And Katerina was lifted to her feet, a strong arm wrapped protectively around her waist. She pulled in a silent breath, staring up at a familiar head of dark hair as a surge of relief warmed her body. But just as quickly as it had come, that relief melted away into the cold night.

"Dylan?"

The arm disappeared. Along with the warmth that came with it.

"Craston?"

The dwarf who'd been about to strike her let out a burst of laughter as Dylan took a step away from Katerina, staring in surprise. One by one, the rest of the deadly gang relaxed their positions, bustling cheerfully forward to shake his hand.

"It's been ages!" The ginger dwarf clapped him cheerfully on the shoulder. Well, he tried. It ended up being more in the center of his back. "Not since that smuggling operation in Kail! You know, the one where you so graciously decided to distract the magistrate's daughter."

The tops of Dylan's cheeks flushed pink as he gave the man a playful shove. "I thought we agreed never to talk about that again."

Katerina stared between them in complete dismay. One second, her rescue had seemed almost inevitable. But now? She'd be surprised if they didn't all decide to go out for drinks!

No, no, no! Don't LIKE him! FIGHT him!

The dwarf straightened the back of Dylan's coat, and she closed her eyes with a grimace.

"Well, what brings you up to these parts?" Dylan finally had the sense to ask, bending down at the same time to return the stray ear-horn. "What're you doing here?"

Yeah, anyone remember me?! The girl in the process of being kidnapped?!

"We were just about to ransom this foreigner," the dwarf replied cheerfully. "And you?"

For the first time, Dylan glanced over his shoulder at Katerina. She was still standing exactly where he'd left her. Arms folded tightly across her thin nightgown. Their eyes met ever so briefly before he turned back to the dwarves—a portrait of ease.

"Actually, I was about to do the same myself."

He...what?! Is he serious?! Not only is he refusing to help me, he's going to ransom me instead?!

Her first instinct was to smack him upside the back of the head. Her second instinct was to kick him once he'd fallen. But something about the look they'd shared made her hold back. There was something more going on beneath the surface. She wouldn't call him an enemy just yet.

"You were?" The ginger dwarf was equal parts surprised and dismayed. "But I thought you were still up north doing—"

"I was," Dylan cut him off quickly. "But that's when I ran into our little friend over here. I saw she came from a wealthy family and was setting out on her own, so I followed her down south."

At which point my farm burned to the ground, taking my imaginary family along with it.

The dwarf's eyes flickered between them. First once. Then twice.

"Well...that's a real shame."

The words sent chills down Katerina's spine, and Dylan quickly lowered his gaze.

"I know," he said apologetically, his eyes flickering surreptitiously around the little circle. "I almost feel bad insisting. But times are hard."

The obvious deference aside, Katerina noticed he slipped into a slightly different accent when he was talking to them. Something that sounded more like their own.

If only it would work.

The dwarf he'd been speaking with frowned deeply, the lines crinkling up the side of his face. While he clearly had the superior numbers, and could most likely win if it came to a fight, he and Dylan obviously had a history. Possibly even a distant friendship.

Katerina held her breath, and unless she was mistaken she could have sworn Dylan's hand drifted ever so casually to the blade by his side.

But a moment later the frown disappeared, and the dwarf's face melted into a friendly smile.

"They most certainly are." He again clapped Dylan on the back, inadvertently buckling the young man's knees. "We'll leave you to it. Sorry about the prior claim."

Prior claim?! Like I'm some kind of property! First come, first serve!

"That's quite all right," Dylan said graciously, taking Katerina by the arm and pulling her back to his side. At a glance, the motion looked very rough indeed, but in reality he couldn't have been more delicate. "Say hi to Bruella for me."

The dwarf nodded in acknowledgement then, one by one, the entire gang disappeared into the night, waving farewell as they went.

Katerina and Dylan stared after them for a long time. A very long time. Neither one could think what to do. Neither one could think what to say. Then, finally, Katerina asked a question.

"Who's Bruella?"

Dylan glanced down at her in surprise, almost as if he'd forgotten she was there. "His wife."

There were a million things to say. A million questions she wanted answered. But at that moment, she couldn't seem to do anything but nod.

"Oh."

They lapsed into silence again, staring out at the cold night. It wasn't until she suddenly shivered that Dylan glanced down at her, his eyes sweeping up and down her thin nightgown. He opened his mouth to say something, but before he could Katerina beat him to the punch.

"So what *are* you doing here?" she repeated the dwarf's question, casting him a sly glance from the corner of her eye. "Unless you really did come to ransom me."

His lips twitched up in the hint of a smile. It was gone before she could see it. "I changed my mind. Decided to come back." It looked like there were several more things he wanted to say, but he shut down instead, suddenly brisk. "And it's a good thing I did. It looks like you can't go more than a few hours without getting into trouble."

Those warm sentiments melted away, and she glared in disbelief. "Are you serious? You actually think this was my fault—"

"Come on, we'll get a different room for the night. Set out in the morning."

He walked off before she could stop him, heading in the opposite direction of the tavern. At this rate, it was for the best. They'd probably demand that she pay to replace the broken door. She picked up her cloak that one of the men must have grabbed and was about to follow, when she saw a crumpled piece of paper on the ground. It had fallen out of his pocket when he charged into the fight. He hadn't noticed it himself.

She cast a quick glance up the street, making sure he wasn't looking, before she scooped it up—reading it in the flickering light of the moon.

I remember a little boy who once needed some help himself...

Katerina's lips parted in surprise, then curved up into the faintest smile as she stared after him in the dark. It seemed the fairies might have been right after all...

Chapter 6

KATERINA STOOD IN THE village square the next morning with a significantly brighter outlook on life. After what had felt like an endless night, the world was bathed in sunlight. The dawn had chased away the shadows. The dawn, or something like it...

"Good morning!" Dylan strode across the damp cobblestones, looking her up and down as he put on his jacket. "Here, I got you a dress. Keep walking around in that nightgown, and people are going to start asking me how much you charge by the hour."

Katerina's smile faded as a wad of fabric flew into her face. She was able to catch it just before it hit the ground. Just in time to see him duck into a bakery and out of sight.

How is it possible to be so grateful and so infuriated at the same time?

Fortunately, the anger faded as she held up the dress, watching it sway back and forth in the morning breeze. It was...pretty. She didn't know how else to say it. Not pretty like her dresses from the castle, but pretty in a simple kind of way. Although it was in the same basic style as the other dresses she saw in the village, this one had avoided the muddy earth tones entirely. It was a robin's-egg blue. Almost the exact same color as the sky.

A little smile crept up her face as her fingers played with white ribbon lacing up the side. If you had asked her three days ago, she wouldn't have been caught dead in it. But now? She didn't know if she had ever been more touched by a simple act of kindness.

"Don't tell me it's not your size."

Katerina looked up with a start as Dylan swept back into the cobblestone square. He was holding a loaf of bread in one hand, and two apples in the other.

"No," she said quickly. "No, it's actually—"

"Because there were only two hanging up on the laundress' clothesline, and the other could have stuffed at least four of you inside."

There was brief pause. Then Katerina's mouth fell open in shock. "Did you...*steal* this dress?"

Dylan glanced over his shoulder then took her by the wrist, pulling her gently in the direction of the forest that bordered the little town. "Of course I stole it. You didn't think I actually went out and *bought* you a dress, did you?" His eyes twinkled at the mere thought, but he picked up the pace as they headed past the local café. "On that note, we'd better get going. Don't want whoever owns it to come running out and see you carrying it away."

Katerina's eyes widened at the thought and she quickly stuffed it under her cloak. Feeling more and more like a petty criminal as she and Dylan hurried down the misty street. Feeling more and more adventurous at the same time...

THERE WAS NO BETTER time for slipping away undetected than in the early morning. Katerina quickly understood why Dylan had insisted they get up so early. There were few enough people out and about that they were able to make good time on the main roads. Only the occasional farmer or miner lifted a distracted hand as they passed by, their minds already focused on a long day's work.

They walked for about an hour without saying a word, and quickly left any stragglers from the village behind them. It wasn't long before they were completely alone. The roads got narrower. The trees got thicker. About ten minutes after that, Dylan gestured to a secluded grove.

"Why don't you get changed? You have to be cold."

Katerina *was* cold. She was freezing, in fact. But she hadn't dared say a single word. She knew the task Dylan was taking on by helping her. And even if he didn't fully understand it, she knew the risk. It was hard enough being a fugitive nowadays without half the royal army after you. The last thing she wanted to do was make his life any harder by slowing them down.

"Thanks," she said quietly, feeling suddenly shy. "That would be great."

Without another word she scampered up into the trees, leaving him behind on the dusty road. Her eyes peered curiously through the gaps in the branches as she quickly peeled off her silky nightgown and slipped the dress over her head instead. She didn't know why she was so shy. For that matter, she didn't know why they were being so quiet. They had shared a room last night—completely alone. A fact that would have made Katerina's royal handlers faint dead away. It was intimate, scary, and very real. And while it could have been incredibly awkward on all counts, it somehow felt as natural as could be.

"Try to get some sleep," he'd advised as he pulled a chair over to the door. "We'll have to set out early tomorrow morning. You'll want all the rest you can get."

Katerina's eyes had flickered to the bed before returning to the chair. He was already settling down, propping up his feet on the nearby dresser, his entire body angled to the door.

"What about you?" she asked quietly, feeling guilty without really knowing the reason why.

She'd had guards before. She'd had people fight for her, chaperone her, stay awake all night to protect her. Why did she feel guilty making this stranger do it now?

Dylan glanced over his shoulder before giving her a swift smile. "I'm fine right here."

In a hard-backed chair? One hand on the armrest, the other on a blade?

Katerina didn't say a word of protest, didn't question his plan. But she did get silently out of bed, padding across the wooden floor to lay a soft hand on his shoulder.

"Thank you," she murmured. "For what you did today. For deciding to come back."

His body had stiffened at the touch, but he didn't turn around. Not for a second. He kept his eyes fixed squarely on the door. Never deviating from his mission. "Get some sleep, princess. We've got a long day tomorrow."

And that was it. That had been all they said. Not until he'd hurled a stolen dress into her face and implied she looked like a prostitute had they spoken again.

Nevertheless, Katerina slept better that night than she had since she'd left the castle. Maybe even before. Secure in the fact that, as long as he was with her, no harm could come. Lulled into the deepest of slumbers by the quiet rhythm of his breath.

But all of that silent solidarity seemed to vanish the longer they were on the road. Maybe it was because of the strange circumstance of their meeting. Maybe it was because they were finally out on the road, exposed and hunted, trying to outrun the darkness that closed in behind.

We need a fresh start. A real introduction. Heck, he doesn't even know my name.

Dylan seemed to be thinking the same thing. The second she walked back out of the trees, her blue dress swishing lightly over the dew-tipped grass, he walked forward with a genuine smile.

"Much better. And now, princess, we can do things properly." Without a word of warning, he offered out his hand. "Dylan Aires. Patron saint of runaways. At your service."

Katerina froze, blinking in surprise. She supposed that in all the time she'd had to think about it, she probably should have come up with some sort of name. But after everything that had happened, she'd given it no more thought than that fateful moment down at the bar.

In the end, she went with a half-truth. A childhood nickname that had faded over time.

"Kat." She took his hand, shaking hesitantly. "Patron saint of nothing. Nice to meet you."

His eyes twinkled as he echoed the words. "Nice to meet you."

She thought that was it, but the introduction didn't end there. Instead of merely shaking her hand, Dylan pulled her in for a sudden embrace. She froze perfectly still as they came together, his hands lingering on her jacket, his face brushing up against her hair.

Truth be told, she really didn't know what to make of it. The man was distant to the point of being cold one moment, and was wrapping his arms around her the next. Sure enough, before she could figure out what was happening, he took a sudden step back, looking almost bored, as if the strange moment had never even happened.

"Well, now that that's settled, we can work out the terms to this little arrangement."

I'm sorry, now that what's settled? And what terms? The fairies didn't say anything about terms.

Katerina shifted nervously, suddenly afraid to meet his eyes. "Okay..."

For his part, Dylan had no trouble looking at her. And he had a way of forcing people to look back at him, whether they wanted to or not. "You want protection, is that right? A safe haven until the danger hanging over your head has passed?"

"Yes, that's right," Katerina answered, feeling more and more anxious all the while.

Dylan paused for a moment, thinking, before suddenly making up his mind. "I'll do it for a price."

A price?! I don't have two shillings to rub together!

Katerina shook her head slowly, trapped in the hypnotic gaze of those eyes. "I have nothing to give you. If I did...it would be different. But I don't have a thing."

He stared at her for a moment before touching the front of her dress. "What about that?"

She froze for a second, then jerked back like she'd been burned, gasping in disbelief. "EXCUSE ME??"

His eyes twinkled but he didn't back down. Instead, he reached out a long finger to catch the chain around her neck, slowly pulling out her mother's pendant.

"That's beautiful," he murmured, his eyes dancing with the magical glow. "And expensive."

"It was my mother's." Katerina's eyes watered involuntarily as she took a step back. "I can't give it away. You can have anything else...but not that."

Dylan's eyes cooled as he slowly lowered his hand. He looked at her appraisingly for a moment before turning on his heel and walking away. "Fine."

He left without a backwards glance. Without even telling her which direction they were headed. Her hand clutched the pendant as silent tears streamed down her face, but just before he disappeared around the bend in the road he glanced back. "Your mother...she'd want you to live, wouldn't she?"

NINE HOURS LATER, KATERINA and Dylan were sitting around a roaring campfire in the middle of the woods. The chain was around his neck. Not hers.

Opportunistic bastard...

She eyed it sullenly, itching to steal it back. Not only had she been forced to give up the one thing left in the world she could call her own, a precious memento of her deceased mother, but it looked as though the necklace was almost happy to be rid of her. Instead of cooling and dulling the way it had when she left the castle, it seemed to glow even brighter the second it touched his skin.

Traitorous pendant...

"You're going to have to get that face of yours under control if you want to make any new friends out here in the woods."

Unlike the princess, Dylan was obnoxiously cheerful. He poked happily at the fire, sending up a spray of sparks, before passing her a stick with a bit of roasted squirrel.

She stared down in complete revulsion, turning up her nose.

"You'll also have to learn to eat when we're lucky enough to find food," he said softly.

She shot him a hostile glare as he propped the stick back up atop the flames. There was probably a point to what he was saying, but at this point she was too irritable to hear it. And furthermore, she'd like nothing better than to wipe that infuriating smile right off his face. "I thought you were going to have to fight those dwarves," she said suddenly, imagining each one of them taking a piece out of him in turn. The thought made her smile.

He flashed her a peculiar look, returning his attention to the fire. "Good thing I didn't. Dwarves are tough fighters. Don't be fooled by their size."

"I won't." The mask of anger fell away as she lifted a hand to the side of her face, wincing as she touched the tender skin where Castor had struck her.

Dylan dropped what he was doing immediately and knelt by her side, frowning sympathetically as he removed her hand and examined it for himself. "You should put some meat on that."

She pulled away in surprise, staring at him like it might be some kind of joke. "Meat?"

A flicker of what looked almost like embarrassment flashed across his face before he pulled back with a scowl, returning to his seat on the opposite side of the fire. "If you don't have ice, raw meat is the best thing. You'll learn that soon enough. Use some of the squirrel."

Katerina matched his scowl with one of her own. "I'm not putting that dead squirrel on my face. And if you don't see anything strange about that statement, you've been living in the woods too long."

"Maybe I have." He gave her a cool smile. "But I'm not the one who's going to wake up with a massive migraine because she was too proud to indulge in a homeopathic remedy."

Before the argument could continue he pushed to his feet, leaving her to either take his advice or not, however she saw fit. She watched as he disappeared into the tent. Waited until he was completely out of sight. Then she grabbed the stick of meat off the fire and tore into it with her teeth, too ravenous to care much where it had come from.

He watched quietly from inside the tent. Never to say a word.

THE PLAN WAS TO GET lost in the woods. Too deep into the wilderness for anyone who could be tracking. Too far off the grid for Katerina's family to ever find her. Of course, she alone knew the truth. She knew they weren't dealing with a trio of vengeful uncles. She knew that her family happened to employ different people to fight their battles.

Assassins, spies, mercenaries, hounds.

With the weight of the entire kingdom behind him, there was very little that her brother couldn't do in terms of finding her and bringing her back to the castle in chains. Or worse.

But as frightening as that possibility was, Katerina had to admit that even Kailas was going to have a hard time finding her with Dylan by her side. It wasn't just that the man set a brutal pace and forced her to follow it twelve hours a day. It wasn't just that he insisted they traipse through every river, trek up every mountain quarry in the hopes of losing her scent.

The man was meticulous.

He was awake by the time Katerina opened her eyes each morning, and was still patrolling the campsite by the time she went to sleep. No detail was too small to escape his attention. No element was too trivial to ignore. Upon seeing a cluster of inexplicably broken branches, he'd once insisted they make a three-day detour, rappelling down the side of some nearby cliffs. When Katerina woke up in the middle of the night, convinced she'd heard a noise, he went on the warpath, combing through every inch of the woods before he came back with a slain raccoon that the two of them proceeded to eat for dinner.

Every move was carefully planned. Every plan was meticulously executed.

But not even the greatest ranger in the world could account for every problem. No matter how hard one tried to ward against it, there were bound to be some mistakes. Like the mistake Katerina walked straight into one balmy afternoon.

It all started when she decided she wanted a bath...

They had been travelling together for two weeks, but despite spending every waking moment together they'd made very little progress in terms of communication. They hardly ever said a word unless they were setting up the campsite. She could count on one hand the number of times she'd heard him laugh. Most of which were at her expense. And yet, a strange sort of familiarity had sprung up between them. A kind of shorthand they were barely aware of themselves.

Yes, the road they shared was incredibly quiet. But it was an attentive kind of quiet. A quiet full of secret looks and hidden glances. A quiet that was slowly driving Katerina insane.

She knew he watched her—same as she watched him. It was part of his job, but even if it wasn't she didn't think the man could resist. Not after he'd pledged to protect her. Even on the rare moments he was out hunting for their food, she still got the feeling he was keeping tabs on her. That he was never very far away.

Of course, that was the very rule she was about to break.

"I'm going for a swim," she declared out of the blue. "There's a river nearby. I'll go now."

Dylan looked up from where he'd been assembling the fire. He knew there was a river nearby, it was where he'd caught the fish he was preparing to cook. But close as it was, he had absolutely no intention of letting her out of his sight.

"The water's freezing," he said dismissively, returning to his work. "You'll hate it."

Nice try. But you can't stop me.

"I'm sure I won't." She pushed to her feet, flashing him a sweet smile. "At any rate, it's not just a swim. I need a bath. And need to wash this dress. It's been days since the last rain."

His hands paused over the kindling as his eyes flickered up to the sky, silently hoping the sun would cloud over and it would start to rain right then and there. When that didn't happen, he pushed to his feet with a sigh. "Look, Kat, I know it's been a long time and we've been moving at a fast pace, but it's just not a good idea for you to go off on your own. I could come with you—"

"Not a chance!" Katerina exclaimed. "I'm going to be *naked*, Dylan. As in, not wearing any clothes. No, you most certainly *cannot* come with me!"

"Well, you're certainly not going alone," he fired back, folding his arms across his chest.

Okay...maybe he can stop me.

She took a step towards the water, weighing her chances of beating him there on foot. But when he raised a single eyebrow, her shoulders wilted with a sigh. "Dylan, it's been weeks," she said quietly, lowering her eyes to the ground. "I know things are dangerous, and I appreciate what you're doing—I really do—but I need a break."

Her defeated tone softened him, as she'd hoped it would, and he glanced back at the river, a worried line creasing down the center of his forehead.

"It's just a dip," she added quickly. "I'll be in and out. I swear."

He hesitated a second more, considering, before his eyes locked on-to hers. "Will you talk to me?"

She blinked, trying to understand. "What?"

"Will you talk to me?" he asked again. "I'll stay far enough away so I can't see anything, but you have to talk to me—the whole time. Let me know you're all right."

Overprotective much?

...not that I should be complaining about that.

"Agreed." Katerina beamed victoriously, thrilled with her success. Not only was she allowed to go on a little excursion, but he'd be forced to break this wretched silence barrier as well. "Now?"

He actually chuckled, glancing down at the half-made fire. The next second he pushed gracefully to his feet, kicking a wave of dirt over the top of it. "Why not."

The princess was so pleased with her impromptu swim in the river that she was unintentionally forgetting a few important things. A tow-el—for one. Leeches, for another. Not to mention the fact that she was going to be having a conversation with Dylan while completely naked.

It might not have seemed like a lot to other people. And judging by what she'd seen at the bar, the man was most certainly used to it. But the castle had certain rules. The royal family had certain rules. And her father, the late king, was nothing short of terrifying in enforcing them. She had never been alone with a man until a few days ago, discounting Alwyn and Kailas. Let alone allowed to go on a two-week-long camp-ing trip, unsupervised in a tiny tent. And while Dylan had been noth-ing but a perfect gentleman, to be honest he seemed borderline disin-terested, she had the sneaking suspicion that this naked jump into the river might change that.

By the time they'd reached the shore, she'd worked herself into a full-on fright.

"You know what?" she began nervously, staring down at the crystalline water. "You were right. This is a bad idea. Let's just head back to camp. I'll help with the fire."

Dylan's eyes danced with amusement as he cocked his head innocently to the side. "Too cold?"

She nodded quickly, grateful for the escape. "Yeah—way too cold."

There was an incriminating pause.

"But you haven't even felt it yet."

An even longer pause. Followed by a guilty, sideways glance.

"I feel like maybe I didn't think this through..."

He laughed shortly before turning abruptly on his heel, heading off into the thick grove of trees. "Relax, princess. You're not my type."

Ridiculous. I've everybody's type.

She glared after him for a moment, kicking off her shoes and turning back to the river. It was a steep climb down, but there were a lot of reeds growing along the side to help her. In only a moment or so she was standing in the frothy surf, which turned out to be pleasantly warm.

"Freezing water, huh," she muttered under her breath. "Yeah, I'm sure I'll hate it."

"What was that?" Dylan called from the trees. "I can't hear you."

A warning to speak up. And to keep talking.

Katerina sighed, then pulled her new dress up over her head, draping it carefully across the rocks so it couldn't get wet. She'd clean it later. For now, she wanted to swim. With a giant smile she pushed out into the open waves, tilting onto her back and staring up at the cloudless sky. "I said I wish the fairies had just given me a guard dog. It would've been a lot easier."

He laughed quietly as he walked through the trees, humming a tuneless melody under his breath. "For you and me both, sweetheart."

She grinned in spite of herself, stretching up an arm to trace nonsense figures into the air. "So you never told me...why did you agree to help me?"

Of course, she'd already seen the note. She already knew that Marigold had created a massive guilt trip out of something in his past. But he didn't know she knew that. He probably didn't realize he'd even lost the note. As far as he was concerned, she was completely in the dark.

"Oh, you know..." He kicked absentmindedly at the pebbles and stones in his path. "An overdeveloped sense of masochism."

She snorted out loud then quickly covered her mouth, glancing nervously at the shoreline. "I'm serious," she insisted, unwilling to let him off the hook. "Why did you come back? You certainly didn't have to—you made that perfectly clear back at the village."

A rather awkward moment of silence followed the statement and Katerina bit her lip nervously, glancing again at the shore. She hadn't meant to make him feel guilty. She simply wanted to know his side. And maybe get him to tell her a little more about himself in the process.

Something he was clearly unwilling to do.

"You ask a lot of questions for a girl on the run," he deflected. "Don't you, *Kat.*"

She froze mid-paddle, staring unblinkingly through the trees. "What the heck's that supposed to mean? You're out of dead rodents to torment me, so you're making fun of my name now?"

"Not in the slightest," he replied. "It's a perfectly lovely name. Is there a last name that goes with it? Or did it burn up with your family farm?"

If I didn't need him so much, I'd kill him myself.

She ducked under the water with a silent scream, then resurfaced in perfect calm. "I'm not even dignifying that with an answer."

He chuckled again. She had the terrible feeling that he could some-how hear the scream. "As long as you answer me something, princess. You need to keep talking."

"Oh yeah?" she shot back. "And what about you? You took my mother's pendant—the most precious thing in the world to me. I've of-ficially bought the *privilege* of traipsing around in the mud with you, except—"

"Except what?"

"—except I don't know a thing about you!" She threw her hands up in exasperation, sending a shower of water droplets shimmering into the sky. "You could be an oversized leprechaun for all I know. A canni-bal who's waiting until the next full moon to eat me alive."

"Right on both counts."

"I'm *serious*." She grinned again in spite of herself, simultaneously hating the way he was always able to make her do that. "Tell me some-thing about *you*. I think I deserve that."

"You paid for protection, princess. Not information. You don't de-serve a bloody thing."

She hesitated, glancing at the shoreline with a coy smile. "All right...I *want* to know."

There was a lengthy pause. Followed by a quiet sigh.

"What do you want to know?"

"Everything," she said immediately, paddling closer so she could better hear. "Start at the beginning. Where are you from? What's your family like? When did you decide to trade in all your mother's good manners and become a thief?"

He laughed again, clear and loud. A contagious, sparkling sound that seemed to echo through the trees. It brightened everything around it, bringing a glowing smile to Katerina's face.

"What makes you think my mother wasn't a thief?" he asked, and she could hear the grin in his voice. "Maybe I was born in a den of thieves. Or to a group of carnival clowns, travelling from village to village. I was in charge of tending to the elephants. This isn't even my true height."

"You really can't do it, can you?" she laughed. "You really can't tell the truth."

"Of course I can."

"Tell me something true."

"One of my limbs is actually a prosthetic."

She burst out laughing again, dunking her head under the water and running her fingers through her silky red hair. By the time she resurfaced he was already in his third or fourth stanza, detailing the nonsensical fallacies of his life. Each as fantastical as the last.

"—at which point I dedicated my time to the study of croquet—"

A sudden noise in the bushes made her jump. Another noise was soon to follow. Dylan was still chattering on obliviously, but whatever it was had been close. And big. And it was far too deliberate not to have been intentional.

Call for Dylan. Call for Dylan!

It was the obvious thing to do. Given the fact that she couldn't fight, it was the only logical option. But in the blind adrenaline that followed, it never even crossed her mind.

Quiet as a mouse, she grabbed her clothes and paddled to the opposite side of the river, climbing out onto the far shore. After quickly slipping the dress over her pale shoulders she crept up the slick bank, holding onto handfuls of the tall grass to help, and out into the sunlit meadow beyond. It was here that she stopped. Looking around. Listening hard. Half convinced she'd imagined the whole thing as her eyes danced with a sea of butterflies.

That's when the world turned upside-down and she flew into the air.

She managed to let out a piercing scream, just the one, before her eyes focused on what had grabbed her and she was stunned silent. Never could she have believed it was possible. Never in her wildest dreams could she have thought it was true. But there he was. Staring right back at her.

A real-life giant.

"Pretty."

He swung her back and forth by the ankle, dangling her at least twenty feet in the air. A wave of nausea crept up her throat and she clapped her hands over her mouth—half to keep from throwing up, half to keep from screaming all over again.

Not that it mattered. Just a few seconds later, Dylan was there.

"Kat?!"

She and the giant heard him shout, and turned toward the river. Rather, the giant turned, and she was swung like a rag doll over the grass. Her dress flew up over her head, and she'd just managed to pull it back down when Dylan raced into the clearing, then skidded to an abrupt stop.

"Crap...that's big."

For a second, he froze in what could only be described as boyish terror. Then he sprinted forward with a fierce shout—fighting it with everything he had. Arrows. Knives. Rocks. Anything that let him keep attacking without getting too close.

It was a valiant effort, but the giant hardly seemed to notice. Quite the contrary. He glanced over curiously, seemed to get annoyed, then lashed out with the back of his hand—swatting, the way one would get rid of a fly. Katerina let out a horrified shriek as Dylan flew seventy feet across the clearing. He landed with a soft crunch in the tall grass, then lay terrifyingly still.

Please let him not be dead! PLEASE let him not be dead!

Katerina was still staring in horror when the giant shook her again, poking at her red hair with a crooked smile. "Pretty."

"Would you stop saying that, you stupid brute!" She smacked his finger away with every bit of strength she had, furious to the point of hysteria. "You might have killed him!"

"Killed?" The giant's face fell with unmistakable remorse as he turned back to look at the fallen warrior. A second later he was plodding across the meadow, crossing it in just three huge steps. He picked up Dylan with a single hand, trying to prop him up as though he was still standing, then let out a miserable sigh when he fell to the ground once more. "Bernie didn't mean to..."

An enormous tear slid down his cheek. Soaking the base of Katerina's dress.

"Bernie?" she asked tentatively. She hadn't seen any blood on Dylan, and it was enough to at least temporarily calm her nerves. "Is that your name?"

The giant nodded at the ground, his bottom lip quivering precariously as more tears slid down his ruddy face. Katerina hastened to reassure him. Half because the tears melted her heart, and half because she was afraid they might unintentionally drown her if they continued to fall.

"My name's Kat. And that's my friend Dylan." She forced her lips up into a smile, trying to cheer the colossus as best she could. "I don't think you killed him. I think he's just asleep."

"Sleep?" The giant squinted curiously at the sun before throwing his head back with ear-shattering laughter. "Now is not the time! There is still light! Silly human!"

"Yeah..." Katerina's eyes watered involuntarily as her ears popped a dozen times. "Silly human. Have you met a lot of us? Humans, I mean?"

Bernie shook his massive head, looking suddenly sad. "They hate Bernie. Call him a monster. Try to burn down his cave."

Katerina stared up in shock, both arms wrapped around his largest finger. "They try to burn down your cave? Even after having talked with you? That's horrible!"

The giant nodded, and sniffed in a way that reminded her very much of a child. The most unlikely of smiles tugged at the corner of her lips, and she suddenly found herself considering the impossible. A second later, she was putting it to words.

"Bernie...could you take us to your cave? Until my friend wakes up, at least?"

To be fair, it's probably not the best idea to voluntarily enter a giant's lair. But with Dylan knocked out cold, she had no way to defend herself. Or him, for that matter. The giant in question seemed nice enough. He might be their only hope.

"You come visit Bernie?"

She nodded tentatively and the giant leapt up into the air, cheering in delight. The earth trembled and shook as they came down, catapulting Dylan's body another ten feet away. She glanced down nervously and beat against his hand with all her might, trying to get his attention. The last thing she needed was to negotiate their safe passage, only to have him accidentally squash her protector in celebration.

"Yes, we'd love to visit Bernie. But you have to let me down first to see if he's okay."

The giant immediately complied, lowering her to the ground with surprisingly delicate hands, then looking around curiously to see where Dylan's body had rolled off to. By the time they found it, he was looking distinctly the worse for wear.

Both Katerina and Bernie flinched at the same time.

"He doesn't like me. Your friend doesn't like Bernie."

Katerina sighed, looping one of Dylan's arms around her neck. "Don't worry. He doesn't like anybody..."

Chapter 7

WHILE KATERINA HADN'T been in a lot of cave-homes to compare them, she had to admit that this one was quite nice. And for a giant's home... she couldn't even begin to allow herself to fathom that this was actually, truly, happening. Bernie had clearly gone out of his way to make things as comfortable and cozy as possible. Scavenging what little he could from campsites, and using flowers and strings of garland to make up the rest. There was a roaring fire in the middle, a pile of wagon covers shoved into the corner to make a bed, even a rudimentary table made from a giant tree stump.

Katerina was propped up on a stool as tall as she was, happily finishing her second bowl of broth. She set it down with a wide smile, licking her lips as she cheerfully applauded the chef. "It was wonderful, Bernie! Thank you so much!" As soon as she'd been sure she wasn't going to be placed *in* the caldron, she'd embraced the idea of dinner wholeheartedly. "Another recipe of your mother's?"

The giant nodded happily, helping himself to second leg of what looked like a giant sort of cow. "She taught Bernie when he was just a baby. Most humans don't know all the spices and yummies you can find in the forest. You just need to know where to look."

They had been talking happily for the last few hours as Dylan lay unconscious upon the hearth. It was a strange meeting, to be sure but, circumstances aside, Katerina had to admit that she was having a fine time. She'd helped him drag the ingredients to the mixing bowl, lobbing them over the side one by one to his fervent applause. She'd perched upon the tip of the spoon as he circled it around and around, trying to explain the finer points of chess. She'd even found the time to drag Dylan further away from the flames when the sleeves of his coat caught fire.

All in all...it had been one of her better days.

A soft moan made them both turn towards the fire. There was a hitch in Dylan's breathing and he was starting to stir, his eyes fluttering open and shut. Katerina set down the piece of mutton she'd been chewing and looked on with interest, while Bernie leapt to his feet.

"He's awake! He's awake! Kat, look—he's awake!"

In his excitement the giant started jumping up and down, waving around his arms in wild delight. Unfortunately, that was the precise moment Dylan opened his eyes for good.

"What the hell??" He yelped, and scrambled backward, only to hit his head on the wall.

"Careful," Katerina said with a sympathetic wince. "Bernie thinks you have a concussion."

Dylan's eyes drifted from the giant to the princess, dilating wide with fear. They took a second more to focus—either from the head wound or from the impossibility of what he was seeing—before he pushed shakily to his feet. One hand went to the wall for balance. The other drifted up to his temple in a daze.

"What in seven hounds is happening right now?"

The giant jumped again, shaking the very stone foundation they were standing on.

"Bernie will get more wood for the fire!" he exclaimed. "Make the cave nice and warm for your friend."

"Oh, that's all right, Bernie," Katerina said quickly. "He really doesn't need special—" She glanced behind her but the giant was already gone, bounding away towards the woods. "—treatment."

The door swung shut behind him, leaving the cave in ringing silence. Katerina looked at Dylan. Dylan looked at Katerina. For a moment, neither one spoke. Then the floodgates opened.

"Who the heck is Bernie? How long was I out? Where the... Where are we?" He paused his rant long enough to glance down at the meat her hand. "...why are you eating a ferret?"

Holy crap, is that what this is? Katerina set it down gingerly and started making her way back to the ground level. It was a laborious process. After she hopped off her stool, she was at a bit of a loss as to what to do next. Bernie had lifted her up onto the high table, and without his giant hands she had to shimmy down the wood face herself, digging her nails into whatever grooves in the bark she could find.

She made it halfway down before her dress caught on a snarl in the wood. A not-so-clever jump later, and her foot got stuck in a crevice. Dylan watched with increasing levels of irritation and restrained sarcasm, and by the time she fell in an undignified pile at his feet he was ready to explode.

"Are you good now?" he asked testily. "You ready?"

Up close, he didn't look nearly as steady as he had from the table. One hand was twitching sporadically against his leg, and the other was half-reaching towards the wall, as if at any moment the blunt-force trauma might catch up and his legs would give way.

"Yes, I am." Katerina straightened herself up with as much dignity as she could muster, trying her very best to project an air of calm. "And to answer your questions, you were only out for a couple of hours and Bernie is the giant you just saw. We're in his house."

There was a beat of silence.

"The giant's name is Bernie?"

Another beat.

"Well...*Bernard*, really." Katerina tossed back her long hair. "But you can hardly expect to be so formal. Not after he invited us over and cooked his mother's soup."

Dylan followed every word, then blinked several times and lowered his eyes to the floor. Not entirely convinced this wasn't all a dream. "...his mother's soup?"

The princess lit up with a bright smile. "Yes, well, you see, Doria had a knack for cooking that she got from her paternal grandfather. So from the time Bernie was just a baby, she tried to—"

Dylan closed his eyes and held up his hand, a wordless plea for silence. It was clearly taking every bit of restraint he had just to control his temper, and when he finally did speak it looked like each word was taking a physical toll.

"Okay..." he began slowly, "you're not from around these parts, so there are certain things you can't be expected to know. One might think common sense would guide you there, but in this case it clearly missed the mark." His eyes flickered back to the cave door before burning into hers with a panicked sort of intensity. "Giants are savage, brutal creatures. Rip you in half for losing at cards kind of brutal. And you're playing house in the middle of its freakin' *cave*??"

"HIS freakin' cave," Katerina corrected angrily. "Don't be rude. I don't discriminate against you just because you're an intolerable street urchin with a penchant for taking things that don't belong to you."

Dylan grabbed the chain around his neck in a muted rage. "This is for services rendered! I didn't steal it!"

"Oh, really." Katerina folded her arms across her chest with a smug smile. "I'm *paying* you to get knocked unconscious by a giant and make me nurse you back to health?"

Dylan's face paled as his eyes flashed in the firelight. "You call this nursing me back to health?"

She resisted the strong urge to stick out her tongue. "I didn't let you catch on fire, did I?"

In what was probably fortunate timing, the door to the outside world swung open again as the giant came back. He had what looked like half the forest piled up in his arms, and without a second thought as to his new little friends he threw it full tilt towards the flickering flames.

Katerina and Dylan dove out of the way just in time.

"Katy?" he called, looking around the cave. "Katy?"

Dylan raised his eyebrows, flashing her an accusatory look as fiery bits of ash rained down around them. "*Katy?*"

He hardly dared to speak above a whisper, and was discreetly pulling them both out of sight behind a fire poker the entire time. Katerina rolled her eyes and tugged herself free, whispering back.

"What? I call him Bernie, but he doesn't get to use a nickname? Be reasonable."

"*Reasonable.*" Dylan made a visible effort to rein himself in. "You're going to lecture *me* about being reasonable when you've landed us straight in the middle of—"

"KATY!"

The fire poker they were hiding behind lifted straight into the air as the giant beamed down at them in delight. He crouched down and laid his open palms upon the floor, but while Katerina climbed right inside—holding onto his thumb for balance—Dylan held back, looking like at any moment the beast might dislodge its jaw entirely and swallow him whole.

"It's okay, Dylan," Bernie reassured him with a toothy smile. "I'll be so careful."

"It knows my name..." Dylan said faintly, backing away into the leg of the table.

Katerina pursed her lips to hide a grin. In hindsight, maybe the giant's smile wasn't so reassuring after all, not when it happened to show every one of his teeth.

"Bernie's just helping us up onto the table, aren't you, Bernie? It's the easiest way to speak back and forth," she explained. "Otherwise he'd have to lie down on the floor."

It seemed so practical when she said it that way, when it was anything but. Her brave young warrior still looked like the world was about to end, but when it became clear that Katerina was going up with or without him, he placed himself hesitantly in the giant's outstretched hand.

"And we're up!"

The two of them jerked violently into the air before grabbing onto his fingers for balance. It wasn't exactly ideal, and by the time they'd found their sea legs they were spilling out onto the table.

"There, you see?" Bernie beamed at Katerina before reaching down ever-so-carefully to pat Dylan on the back. He was clearly being as delicate as possible, even when he accidentally knocked him over a fork. "It's not so bad."

As Katerina smothered a fit of laughter behind her hand, Dylan caught himself gracefully and spun around to look the giant in the eye. Whatever was going through his head, battling a lifetime's worth of experience must have been extraordinary. Because, after a lengthy appraisal, he nodded his head with a little smile.

"Not so bad."

Bernie started smiling so hard Katerina thought his face might burst. Then his eyes welled up with tears, and she hurried forward to hold his hand. Life for something as ostracized and feared as a giant had to be very lonely. Especially so far out in the woods. She and Dylan had left the road behind more than eight days ago. No one came so deep into the forest. It was basically abandoned.

At least, it was supposed to be. But it apparently wasn't tonight.

"Bernie is so glad he made new friends," the giant wailed, trying and failing to keep his emotions under control. "Such good humans. Not like the bad ones."

Katerina stroked his hand sympathetically, while Dylan stepped forward with a little frown.

"The bad ones?" he repeated.

In a flash, his entire face transformed. No longer was he the weather-hardened ranger, secretly plotting how to impale the giant and make his great escape. He was an open book. A shoulder to lean on. A gentle soul. If Katerina hadn't been so disturbed by the whole metamorphosis, she might have been seriously impressed.

"What bad ones, Bernie?" he asked kindly, silently pleading for more information. "Did you meet some of them tonight?"

Bernie shook his head fearfully. A fairytale monster who didn't know his own strength. "Not tonight. But there are bad tracks in the woods. Made by bad things."

An image of her brother's hell hounds flashed through Katerina's mind, and she stepped closer to Dylan with a shudder. Was it really possible? Had they somehow picked up on their trail?

"What kinds of things?" she asked fearfully.

It was the giant's turn to shudder.

"Bernie doesn't want to say."

She glanced at Dylan for help, but the man said nothing. His eyes merely flickered out to the darkness, looking decidedly grim. In the end, it was up to her to lift spirits.

"Well...you don't have to say anything, Bernie." She forced a cheerful smile, stopping the giant's tears before they could begin. "You're right. You made some good new friends today."

It was the right thing to say. The second she said it, the tears in Bernie's eyes vanished completely, replaced with the brightest of smiles. "Yes, Kat and Dylan are my friends, and Dylan was *not* killed, and would he like some soup?"

One sentence ran into the next, and it took Dylan a second to realize he'd been asked a question. "What? No, that's...I'm fine. Thank you," he added hastily, in an effort to be polite. And to stay alive.

"You should really try some," Katerina urged. "He's actually a much better cook than you."

Dylan flashed her a chilling look, and she raised her hands innocently.

"I'm just saying...squirrel isn't for everyone."

Bernie obviously took the hushed argument to mean a 'yes', and snatched up a giant knife to chop up some more parsley. Dylan closed his eyes with a shudder as the blade whipped through the air, just inches above his head. When he opened them again, he was looking rather green.

"I think I'm going to be sick..."

"That's the spirit." Katerina clapped him cheerfully on the back, lowering her voice to a conspiratorial whisper. "But not until after the soup."

THE NEXT MORNING, DYLAN and Katerina set out as soon as he was able to walk in a straight line. They were laden with gifts from their own personal friendly giant. Tubs of berries and butter. A loaf of bread the size of a small horse. Even a cache of herbs from his garden.

They thanked him profusely and dragged it all away with cheerful smiles until he was out of sight. Then they set it on the ground in front of them, and took stock of what could be used. While the sentiment was incredibly sweet, they simply didn't have enough strength, or enough limbs, to lug around a giant-sized portion of food. So after packing everything they could possibly carry, they sat down beside a giant waterfall and proceeded to feast on the rest.

"I'm not going to lie," Katerina said between mouthfuls of biscuit, "this is a lot more what I had in mind when you said we'd be living deep in the woods."

Dylan spread a helping of butter across his toast with the tip of his hunting knife, chuckling all the while. "Biscuits and tea? Someone got used to the finer things back on the farm."

She tensed for a moment, then let it go. It had become clear over the course of their travels that both of them had secrets. But as long as he wasn't spilling his, she kept hers close to the vest.

"And what about you?" she asked with a rueful grin. "You used to the finer things?"

Dylan licked the butter off the blade before sticking it back in his jacket. "Clearly."

"I'm serious," she giggled, "you may act like this rough and tumble mountain man, but there are some things that you can't hide. Literary references. Patterns of speech." She cocked her head curiously, looking him up and down. Just the other day, he'd sarcastically quoted the Gutenberg Bible. "You've clearly been educated. How did that come about? For a travelling thief, I mean."

He flashed her a grin. "I thought we agreed I wasn't a thief."

She grinned back. "Stop dodging the question."

Perhaps it was the sudden abundance of food. A luxury that can't possibly be overstated for two slightly malnourished people living in the woods. Perhaps it was the fact that they'd recently walked unharmed out of the cave of a giant. But something had loosened his tongue.

He set down a bottle of cider as the grin faded slowly from his face. It faded into something thoughtful. Something almost nostalgic.

"My mother taught me," he said quietly. "My father wanted me to get a tutor, which was the custom at the time. But she wanted to teach me herself. Science and mathematics. History and literature. Whatever she could get her hands on. It was all there."

His eyes warmed for a moment, softening with a tenderness that Katerina had never seen before. She couldn't help but soften in return. "Where is your mother now?"

Just like that, the tenderness faded. The warm light vanished from his eyes.

"She's dead," he answered bluntly. "Both my parents are dead."

That was the end of the conversation. Neither one of them said anymore. A few minutes after they'd finished Dylan pushed to his feet, surveying the remaining supplies with a trained eye. "We should haul these down to the nearest village, see what kind of price we can get."

Katerina looked down in surprise, then realized the obvious practicality of his words. "Oh. Right." She'd been planning on merely leaving it. A gift to the forest creatures.

Stop thinking like a princess, and start thinking like a fugitive. Waste not, want not.

"There's one just a few miles down the road." He squinted through the trees, trying to gauge the distance. "We should make it there before noon. Can you take the cider?"

"Yeah." Katerina scooped up the leather straps and flung the bottles over her shoulder. The second they were balanced she grabbed up the deerskin blanket they used in the tent, as well as whatever cooking supplies she could manage before slipping them quickly into her pack. The cloak was the next to go on. Hair back. Hood up. The bottom of it tucked safely into the tops of her boots so it wouldn't drag—a lesson she'd learned the hard way after getting stuck in some brambles.

It was a necessary routine, but a quick one. She didn't realize Dylan was staring at her until she'd already made it to the bottom of the hill.

"Well, look at you." His eyes twinkled as he brushed a stray lock of hair away from her eyes, tucking it safely back into her hood. "A seasoned traveler. Even survived your first giant."

She blushed with embarrassment, but couldn't resist a small smile. "It helped that he gave me soup."

Dylan laughed shortly, then shook his head—staring off into the horizon. "It helped that he gave you soup..."

Chapter 8

ALTHOUGH KATERINA WOULDN'T have believed it just a few weeks before, her legs had become conditioned for a mountain hike. They made it into the village well before noon, and were able to set up an impromptu stand to sell their remaining food before the local workmen came back from the mines for lunch. As fresh-made jam and butter were in short supply, especially the delicious ones Bernie had provided, they sold all their wares quickly and were left counting their coins.

"Not bad," Dylan murmured, slipping a handful of bronze into a leather pouch inside his jacket. "Not quite enough for what we need to buy...but it's close."

"And what exactly is it that we need to buy?" Katerina asked, sticking close to Dylan as she dodged the usual curious stares from the townsfolk.

Strangers were seldom seen in those parts; towns tended to act as giant families, and any traveler from the outside world was news indeed. Let alone travelers that looked like her and Dylan.

Sure enough she heard the telltale giggling, and looked up to see a group of blushing girls hurry past, casting him secret looks as they whispered behind their hands.

"I need a new handle for my hatchet. It split up the middle when that flippin' giant threw me across the field. And you need a new a pair of shoes. Proper hiking ones."

Katerina turned to him in surprise, automatically glancing down at her tiny feet. While the rest of her wardrobe might have changed, she was still wearing the same dainty slippers as when she'd left the castle, and they weren't holding up well to the mountain terrain. "Oh, I didn't..." She trailed off, not knowing quite what to say. "I mean, can we afford something like that?"

A little grin crept up the side of his face as he continued packing the supplies they'd be taking with them. "I think we can splurge just this once. Heaven knows I love shoe shopping."

Katerina let out a giggle, which was soon echoing across the town square. She looked over again to see the same group of girls still watching, hiding behind the door of the local pub. She resisted the urge to roll her eyes and was about to get back to work, when a sudden question occurred to her. One she hadn't thought to ask until that very moment. "Dylan...do you have a girlfriend?"

He almost dropped the bag he was holding. Those blue eyes of his shot up in surprise before hastily lowering back to the ground. "What do you mean?"

A mischievous smile danced in her eyes, and she suddenly found herself highly interested in his response. "It isn't a difficult question. What part of it didn't you understand?"

"No, I... uh... meant, why are you asking me?"

This time it was Katerina's turn to suddenly not know where to look, taken aback by the directness of the question. She fumbled for a moment, before the girls giggled again and she found her escape. "I'm just saying...you're breaking a lot of hearts over there. The least you could do is show them some skin. Do a little dance or something."

He glanced towards the pub in surprise, noticing the girls for the first time, before returning to his work with a look of complete indifference. "A dance, huh? Show some skin?"

She flashed him a grin and tightened the strap on her bag. "If nothing else, we may be able to get some more coin—"

"Princess Katerina?!"

She and Dylan froze at the same time. Eyes fixed on the ground. Every muscle hardening perfectly still. They were facing away from whoever had spoken, and without turning around it was impossible to gauge how bad the situation might be.

One guard? A dozen?

Katerina's heart pounded behind her eyes as a strange tingling sensation started spreading up the base of her neck. She was going into shock. It was easy to recognize, but hard to avoid. At any rate, she didn't have time to be shocked right now. She needed to breathe. She needed to think.

"But I thought she was older than the prince. That they were twins, but she was born first."

Wait... what?

The icy panic holding the princess loosened its grasp just enough that she was able to turn around. That she was able to glance over her shoulder and see the two farmers talking behind her.

"I thought so, too, but I guess not." The taller of the two men folded his arms authoritatively, then spat on the ground. "If Kailas is on the throne, he has to be the rightful heir."

The rightful heir.

Just hearing the words was enough to make her blood boil. The image in front of her started pulsing with rage, and she was about to lose herself entirely when a hand clamped down on her arm.

"Kat?"

She jumped like she'd been burned, and looked up to see Dylan standing in between her and the farmers.

He was staring down at her with a very strange expression on his face. A mixture of concern and a sort of abstract caution she didn't fully understand. He studied her for a moment, trying to decide what to say, when he cocked his head suddenly to the main road. "There's another village just a few miles from here. They might have what we need." His dark hair spilled across his forehead as he stared into her eyes. "Do you want to leave?"

It was a strange question. One made even stranger by the fact that they were already in a village, and just over his shoulder she could see rows upon rows of little shops.

But in that specific moment, none of that seemed to matter.

Katerina took one more look at the farmers behind her. One more look at the chain circling around Dylan's neck. And she suddenly couldn't stand to be in the town any longer. "Yes." She pulled her arm away and stormed up the street. "Let's go."

They left without a backward glance. Without a word between them. But it wasn't until the little village was far behind them that Katerina realized the obvious question.

She knew why she had frozen.

But why had Dylan frozen, too?

THEY HIKED THE FOUR miles to the next village in relative silence. Either unwilling or unable to address what had transpired in the marketplace. Oddly enough, it was Dylan's silence that frightened Katerina more than anything else. More than questions, or accusations, or even carrying on as though nothing had happened. Because something *had* happened. She just didn't know what.

Fortunately, she didn't have long to wait. Before it would have seemed possible, a chorus of familiar sounds echoed up the road. The sound of people laughing, people talking, people bargaining as they haggled over things to buy. Both she and Dylan came to a simultaneous pause before proceeding onward at the same time. Moving with an instinctual synchronicity. Never more than a few inches of space between them. As two travelling companions alone in the world tended to do.

"Now *this* is more like it."

They stopped at the top of a hill, looking out over the encampment in the canyon below. It was an outdoor market on wheels. A giant, multi-colored extravaganza. Teeming with life. Bursting with activity. But that wasn't all there was to it. For a second, Katerina simply stared. Then her eyes widened as she began to slowly process what she was seeing.

"None of them..." She trailed off, feeling very much like she'd stepped out of the real world and into one of her childhood storybooks. "None of them are human."

Indeed, they were everything but.

Dwarves were peddling their treasures. Trolls and pixies were working side by side. There were clusters of fairies selling nectar from a high-hanging row of potted plants, and a pack of shifters was challenging everyone who walked past to arm wrestle (after inadvertently consuming all the ale they'd been intending to sell). Scores of witches, and goblins, and vampires, and nymphs were wandering from booth to booth. At times they'd pause to make a purchase. At times they'd pause to flirt. But most often they simply wandered around. Chattering noisily. Drinking heavily. Completely isolated from the rest of the world in the safety of their own little bubble.

Carnival of freaks.

"*This* is where we're going?" Katerina asked, failing to understand Dylan's enthusiasm. While she might be literally aching to see some of the creatures up close, after her last encounter with the supernatural world she was more than a little hesitant to venture any closer. "Down there?"

He felt her stiffen, and glanced down with a crooked smile. "Relax. I can feel you stressing from here. Just stay close, and you'll be fine."

Yeah, or maybe I'll be attacked by vampires. Or kidnapped by dwarves. Stranger things have happened. Like, VERY recently.

She put her hands on her hips and tried her best to sound reasonable. "You do realize that we're going to stand out, right?"

A look of anticipation danced in his eyes as he took her by the wrist and started leading her down the hill. "In this crowd...what better way is there to blend in?"

What better way indeed?

As ironic as it was, Dylan was right. No one gave them a second glance as they wandered through the bustling market. There was simply too much else to see. There were fire-breathers and baton-twirlers. Contortionists, and a woman who looked suspiciously as though she might be part bird. Everywhere you looked, there was something new and exciting. Katerina was so spellbound that she hardly realized someone was talking to her until a wrinkled hand grabbed her by the wrist.

"Such beautiful eyes you have, my dear."

She looked down in surprise to see the most ancient, mottled, semi-terrifying lady she'd ever seen. Her yellowing fingernails were long enough to curl. Her beady eyes seemed to pierce right through the princess' skin. And her brittle white hair framed a face so overtaken by a hooked-nose that there was little room for anything else. But, despite being born sometime in the Stone Age, she was nothing if not strong. Already, the tips of Katerina's fingers were starting to turn blue.

"I'm...I'm sorry?"

A hag, she suddenly realized. *This must be a hag.*

She elbowed Dylan discreetly in the ribs to get his attention, while the hag took a step closer, curling a crooked finger around the princess' cheek. Katerina shuddered at the touch.

"You have such beautiful eyes," she repeated, a hungry look flashing in her own. "I'll give you twenty shillings for the left."

"For the left..." Katerina trailed off, her face paling in horror. "For my left eye?!"

A strong hand pulled her backward, out of the hag's grasp.

"No, thank you," Dylan said sweetly.

A second later, he was tugging her down the street. The old woman melted into the crowd, pouting, as Katerina struggled clumsily to keep pace. She couldn't help flashing continual looks over her shoulder, as if at any moment the crone might reappear and demand her right eye as well. "Did you just..." she panted in shock, clawing at his arm, "...did you just hear what she—"

"Yeah, I did." He came to a sudden stop, far too preoccupied with his own problems to care much about hers. "Take it as a compliment. In the meantime, we're going to need a bit more money than what we have now."

Katerina waited for further elaboration, but none came. Instead he fell silent, levelling her with an expectant stare. She stared back for a moment, waiting, before flashing a sarcastic smile. "Well, why don't I just run down to the magical money store and get some?"

"That's hilarious." He didn't crack a smile. "But not exactly what I had in mind. Do you have any skills? Cooking? Sewing? Singing? Anything at all that could be of use?"

Perhaps he didn't realize how condescending he sounded, or perhaps he did. With Dylan, it was hard to tell. Katerina folded her arms defensively over her chest, eyes narrowing with a glare. "Do *you* have any useful skills?" she fired back.

"I most certainly do." Without further ado, he raised his voice and called out over the crowd. "Does anyone here need someone killed?"

Katerina's mouth fell open in shock as the creatures nearest to them glanced over curiously, then talked amongst themselves. She'd thought it was some kind of terrible joke, but not a moment later a springy little man in a giant sunhat waved his hand about excitedly.

"I do! I have someone I need killed!"

"Perfect." Dylan nodded at the man, then handed Katerina a shilling. "Take this, get us both some lunch. I'll be back within the hour."

"You have got to be joking!" she exclaimed.

He frowned at the coin before glancing at the pub. "It won't be more than that."

"No! I mean about the—"

"Gotta go." He swung his pack over his shoulder as the little man eagerly weaved his way through the crowd. "One hour. Don't go wandering off by yourself. Stay at the pub."

Katerina quickly slipped the shilling into her pocket, fighting the rising panic in her chest. "But I thought we were supposed to stick—"

A second later, he was gone.

"—together."

Her shoulders wilted as she was left standing perfectly still in the middle of the bustling crowd. Then her head turned towards the pub and she started trudging forward with a quiet sigh.

"They'd better have biscuits..."

AFTER HER LAST VISIT to a tavern, Katerina had learned to be cautious. After being stolen by a band of thugs away from said tavern, that caution had developed into a healthy fear.

She sat at a private booth in the back corner, where she had a good view of the action without really being a part of it. It was a wise decision. Over the course of the next hour, she witnessed no less than nine fights, five dance-offs, and one very uncomfortable proposal.

A dwarf drunkenly serenaded a nymph. A shifter proudly proclaimed he could turn into the 'king of beasts' before accidentally shrinking into a hedgehog. And unless Katerina was very much mistaken, the same troll she'd seen dancing in the first tavern was dancing here as well—eyes closed with a beatific smile on his face as he swayed back and forth to a melancholy ballad.

And this is why we're supposed to stick together...

As it neared the hour mark, Katerina got up from the table and made her way up to the bar to order some food. They seemed to have a wide selection, but she had yet to see anything remotely edible for humans. Although a part of her dearly wanted to order Dylan some scarab shells just to see the look on his face.

"What'll it be today, miss?"

Her eyes flickered up to the bar as a man with three too many arms wiped off the counter while simultaneously offering her a menu. She took it quickly, not wanting to stare, and ordered the first thing innocuous enough for her to recognize.

"Two sandwiches and two ciders please." She lay her money upon the counter and tapped her fingers nervously as he disappeared into the kitchen. It had only been about thirty seconds since she'd gotten up from her table, but already she was getting 'the eye' from no fewer than seven different men seated around the bar.

Don't accept drinks from anyone, and don't let anyone drink you. Rules to live by.

To *live* by is right.

When Katerina finally chanced a peek around, she saw a man grinning at her from the end of the bar. A grin that was made all the more feral by the two giant fangs hanging all the way down to his collar. The man by his side wasn't much better. He was suave enough to blow a kiss, but when he turned to the side Katerina could have sworn she saw a pair of gills.

She stifled a shudder and took the tray of food as soon as it was offered. With a hasty "keep the change," she swiftly headed back to the table, keeping her head down and her eyes locked firmly on the floor.

If only it was enough.

"Well, hello there!"

The tray vanished right out of her hands, disappearing into thin air. Her lips parted with a gasp, and she jerked up her chin to see the tallest man in the world smiling down at her. At a first glance, he seemed to be all limbs. Legs as long as her body. Arms that stretched down to the floor. But upon closer inspection, he was actually quite small. The impressive height, as well as everything else about him, was nothing but an illusion. The same sort of illusion that had stolen her lunch.

"Hello yourself," she snapped, her temper getting the better of her. She'd watched these hooligans long enough to have no patience with them now. "Want to give me back that tray?"

He lowered to the floor with a toothy grin. "What's the hurry? I've been watching you for a while, you know. The most beautiful girl in the village." He curled his finger through the air, and a sprig of flowers popped into his hand. "I was hoping we might spend a little time together..."

"Absolutely not!" She swiped the flowers away and cast them to the floor. "Now give me back that tray before I—"

"Before you what?" he taunted playfully, thrilled that she was talking to him no matter how angry her tone. "You know, I think you're even cuter when you're mad."

Oh, that's it!

Without stopping to think, she swung her fist towards his face. It was a strong punch. One that came with absolutely no warning. She might have made contact, too, if the man hadn't seen it coming and vanished into the air. The second he was gone his magic went with him. The flowers disappeared while her tray popped back into sight, sitting innocently on her table.

"That's right, you'd better run!" she gloated, smoothing down her dress. Those who had seen the altercation lifted their hands with a polite smattering of applause, further boosting her rapidly inflating ego. "You have to use force with upstarts like that," she said authoritatively, wishing very much that Dylan had been there to see her success. "Little coward—"

If only she had stopped there. But ever since her father was murdered and she was chased out of her rightful kingdom by a pair of hellish dogs, the princess was stuck with the very worst luck.

Her foot caught on the edge of a table, and her dress twisted around her legs. Less than a second later, she was falling in what felt like slow motion. Falling right...*through* one of the patrons?

She let out a frightened shriek as the man flashed her a cartoonishly-somber look. But just like clockwork, a strong hand came out of nowhere and caught her a second before she hit the floor.

"Making friends, I see."

She straightened up to see Dylan staring down at her with a beaming smile. There was a flush of color to his cheeks and a windswept look of triumph about him. It only made things even worse.

"I wasn't..." Her cheeks blossomed bright red as she gestured back to the tray. "If you must know, I was actually teaching these good people a lesson about...holy hot-sticks!" She both forgot and remembered all at once. "That man! Dylan, I think that I actually—"

"—went through him. Yeah, you did."

She paled in horror as she glanced back to where he was still sitting, but Dylan merely flashed the man a cheerful smile. A smile that was absolutely not returned.

"Don't worry about Lester—he died ages ago. Hardly even notices anymore." The translucent outline of the man seemed to shimmer in rage as Dylan grinned again. "You all right, Lester?"

The ghost flipped him off and returned his eyes to the table, staring longingly at an untouched drink. Dylan waved obliviously and led Katerina back to their table.

"Yeah, he's great..." She stared at him in shock as he settled down at the booth—tearing into his sandwich with the hunger of a thousand men—before perching tentatively beside him. He might be unaware of the giant elephant in the room, but she was unable to let it go so easily. And, no, it wasn't the ghost.

"Did you really just kill someone?"

There was a pause in the eating. Followed by a splash of cider.

"Not *someone* so much as...*something*." He lifted his arms and looked down in disgust at a thick layer of green ooze covering the front of his jacket. "That'll take ages to clean..." A rather mournful expression flitted across his face before he lit up again. "But hey, I got the new hatchet I needed as well as some shoes for you. They're in my pack—I'll show you later."

So many questions. So little time. But, strangely enough, now that the world had settled back on its axis and the two of them were reunited, eating sandwiches, it was a different question entirely that rose to the princess' lips. "What did you mean earlier? When you said I wasn't your type?"

Dylan choked on a piece of bread and washed it quickly down with a drink. He resurfaced a moment later with an unexpected smile. "Where the heck did that come from?"

Katerina grinned guiltily, pushing her sandwich around on her plate. "I was just wondering. I mean, when you asked me earlier today if I had any skills, if I could do anything useful..." She trailed off, the smile melting off her face. "Do you wish you hadn't agreed to this?"

He froze a moment in absolute surprise before setting the sandwich back on his plate. "Kat, I never wanted to give you the impression that—"

"Because I get it," she said quickly. "You've been out on your own for longer than you can probably remember. You know how to live off the land. You know how to fight. You can take care of yourself." A sudden pang tightened her chest. She didn't realize how jealous she was of those words until she said them out loud. "It isn't any wonder that someone like me isn't your type."

His lips parted as a very strange expression flickered across his face. One that bore a strong resemblance to that soft tenderness she'd seen back in the woods. It was gone before she could say for sure. Replaced with an enchanting smile. "Yes, except that's not what I meant in the slightest." His eyes twinkled as he took a deep drink of his cider. "Beautiful, inquisitive, resilient, stubborn...that's not my type at all."

THE TWO OF THEM FINISHED eating as quickly as possible and made their way out of the outdoor marketplace, heading back to the main road. Dylan told her quietly over their food that he'd heard rumors and bits of idle talk that groups of strange men had been combing the countryside—working their way deeper and deeper away from the kingdom. While the news hardly came as a surprise, especially after what the giant, Bernie, had seen, it was plenty of motivation for them to get out of the open and into the woods.

"I still can't believe you bought me shoes," Katerina murmured as they headed past a caravan of shifters and goblins who'd set up shop on the side of the road. "The mighty Dylan Aires, shopping for women's footwear. I certainly hoped you remembered that red is *out* this season—"

A low whistle interrupted her teasing, and the two of them glanced over to see trio of shifters gawking appreciatively from the side of the road. They may have looked like men on the outside, but whatever beast lay within had most certainly endowed them with strength. Even hidden beneath their clothing, Katerina could see the thick, muscular arms. Their powerful frames leaning casually against the side of a wagon, an assortment of needless weapons dangling from their belts.

"Well, aren't you the luckiest man in the kingdom?" The tallest one called to Dylan, peeling himself away from the wagon and walking towards them with a surprisingly friendly smile. "I don't know if I've ever seen such a pretty girl in person. She yours?"

Am I...his?! What the heck kind of place is this?!

Dylan avoided the question but smiled back, keeping things intentionally light and cheerful. "Where are you folks headed?"

By now, the other shifters had joined them and a group of goblins came out as well, each one looking Katerina up and down before joining in the conversation.

"We heard there was a market nearby." The man gestured to the wagons behind him, each one filled to the brim with everything from food, to clothing, to blankets, to blades. "Thought we might try our luck. See if we can unload any of this merchandise."

And I wonder where you got that merchandise. Katerina's eyes flickered over the wagons, suddenly convinced that everything she was looking at was either stolen or forged.

Dylan obviously thought so, too, but he kept a smile on his face and his opinions safely to himself. "I'm sure you will. The place is packed."

"You just came from there?" The shifter pretended to be surprised, although it was clear they'd been walking down the road. "Shame. We were hoping we might entice you to trade. The girl for some food?" he asked coaxingly. "Or maybe a new blade to keep you occupied?"

Are they freakin' serious?!

Both she and Dylan stiffened at the same time, although he kept his face a perfect mask of calm. For a second he raised a teasing eyebrow, pretending to consider, before refusing outright.

"If only I could." He wrapped a deliberate arm around her waist, pulling her closer in an unmistakable display of possessiveness. "But I'm afraid I can't do without her." His eyes flashed to her face, twinkling with the hint of a secret smile. "She's indispensable."

For a split second, she was terrified they were going to take her by force. Terrified that the entire encounter would dissolve into a bloodbath that neither she nor Dylan would be able to walk away from. But the shifter in charge merely threw his head back with a laugh.

"Like I said...it's a shame." He lifted a hand to wave, while simultaneously signaling for the wagons to keep moving. "Safe travels. And please come find me...if you ever change your mind."

Dylan's arm tightened around her waist as he forced a tight smile of farewell. It wasn't until the first wagon had passed them by that he dared to release her. And even then, she maintained a close distance as they walked through the tiny crowd. Dylan didn't seem to mind. Men and goblins parted in front of them as they cut through, but they got their fair share of whispers and stares. At one point, Katerina could have sworn an especially brazen goblin grabbed Dylan's derrière as they walked by.

It didn't matter. He kept moving. Never slowing down. Never making direct eye contact with anyone they passed. It was a good strategy. The only strategy that was guaranteed to keep them both alive apparently. And it worked, too.

It worked all the way until a drunken shifter near the back of the group reached out and caught the edge of Katerina's skirt.

Dylan had him up against a wagon before she could even turn around. His face pale with rage and the edge of his knife pressed against the man's throat.

"Dylan, no!" she gasped, but it was too late.

The second the rest of them heard the commotion, the caravan stopped in place. Within seconds, the shifter they'd been speaking to—the one in charge—hurried to the back of the group, stopping short in surprise when he saw the scuffling pair by the wagon.

"What the heck is this?!"

Dylan glanced over his shoulder, but the knife didn't move an inch. "I'd assumed when you bid us safe travels that you were being sincere. That we could pass through without harm." He spoke through gritted teeth, visibly fighting the urge to cut the shifter in half. "I'd assumed that your word carried the authority for the rest of the group. Perhaps I was mistaken."

Katerina's eyes shot to the man in terror. It was a brilliantly worded explanation, one that required their release in order for the man to save face. She just wasn't sure that kind of logic would work on people who lived in such a manner. The kind who were always itching for a fight.

She underestimated their pride.

"You were *not* mistaken."

The man strode forward and ripped Dylan's knife away with his bare hands. The shifter pinned against the wagon gasped in relief, but no sooner had he done so than his own leader grabbed him by the throat—punching him three times in quick succession. He crumpled to the ground without a sound. Eyes sealed shut. Out cold.

"And you will have no other problems. I assure you."

His eyes flashed as he cocked his head towards the open road. It was a welcome dismissal, but a curt one. If Dylan hadn't so publicly challenged his authority, there would most likely have been a different man lying on the ground.

And Katerina wouldn't be leaving anytime soon.

She stood staring, her breath caught in her throat.

Dylan said not a word. He just nodded swiftly and grabbed Katerina by the arm, pulling her down the road at such a pace it was all she could do to keep from breaking into a jog. They didn't slow down until the wagons were far behind them. Even then, they kept up a steady clip until they'd lost themselves in the greenery of the woods. It was only then that Dylan suddenly released her, spinning around so that he could examine her for himself.

"Are you all right?" he asked softly, looking her up and down while avoiding her eyes.

She nodded mutely. Now that the danger was behind them, she was far more interested in Dylan's reaction than anything the shifters had done.

Indispensable, was she? Impossible to live without?

"I'm sorry I couldn't do more," he muttered, still avoiding her gaze. "But with so many of them and just the two of us...I couldn't see a way to kill the man while keeping you safe."

Perhaps it's because I'm beautiful, inquisitive, resilient, and stubborn...

"At any rate, I don't imagine we'll be seeing them again." He took a step back, squinting up at the mid-afternoon sun. "Bands like that usually travel... they usually... why are you smiling?"

It was true. Despite everything that had just happened, Katerina was standing there with a giant smile plastered on her face. She didn't answer him. She didn't say a word. She simply took a step forward, stretched up on her toes, and gave him a kiss on the cheek.

"Thank you for the shoes."

Chapter 9

"I'M TELLING YOU THE truth!" Katerina exclaimed. "The guy had to be at least nine feet tall! He vanished our sandwiches into thin air, challenged me to some sort of duel, then pulled out a sword!"

Dylan kept his eyes on the ground, a faint smile playing about his lips. "A sword, huh? Sounds intense."

The two had been walking for the last three hours, mostly uphill, straight into the heart of the forest, losing themselves in the emerald trees. It had been a difficult journey, filled with steep ravines and mountain climbs, but their spirits were surprisingly high. The longer the journey, the taller the tales. When Katerina had started telling Dylan about the tavern twenty minutes earlier, she had more or less stuck to the facts. By now, the magician was a near-giant. The sprig of flowers had turned into a blade. And the flirting had escalated to a full-out declaration of war. After kissing his cheek earlier she still touched her lower lip periodically, swearing she could still feel the faint roughness of his chin. He needed a shave. It had been a few days, and there was a light shadow now showing on his jawline. It made him more rugged, more—

Enough! She wasn't interested. He was a thief. Taking her mother's necklace. He was only doing what he needed to because a deal had been struck. And after the last near altercation with the shifters... She forced herself to take a deep breath. He'd only done what he had to in order to protect his own hide, not hers.

At least, that's what she kept telling herself.

Where was she again on her story about the pub? When Dylan had so irresponsibly left her alone?

"It *was* intense!" Katerina's eyes were wide as saucers. By now, she was half-believing the story herself. "So, anyway, he swung at me a couple times—nothing I couldn't handle. But before he could strike the final blow, I back-flipped over his head."

"I thought he was nine feet tall."

"...I'm a world-class jumper."

They exchanged a quick look, and she stared at his cheek where she'd kissed him before the story continued anew.

"By the time he turned back around, I was ready." Katerina lifted her fists in the air, enthusiastically miming a fight that never happened. "One punch to the nose—that's all it took. The guy went down hard. Took half the tavern down with him. He may have cracked the floor."

Dylan nodded practically, reaching out to help her over a fallen log. "And that's when you tripped through Lester?"

Ah, yes, she'd forgotten about that little part.

She accepted his hand automatically, chewing on her bottom lip as she stalled for time. Keep telling the story, when he knew the ending, or focus on the warmth of his touch? In the end, she decided it was probably best to just change the subject.

"So what about you?" she asked casually. "How did you get covered in green slime?"

He grimaced automatically as he remembered, sending a simultaneous tremor through his hands. "That's a story for another time. But I'm glad you enjoyed the market. Aside from that old woman trying to take your eyes, I think the whole thing was a huge success."

How could I have possibly forgotten about that? My life has gotten so strange. Katerina nodded fervently, her mind racing as she played back the events of the day. Yes, there were some near-misses. And yes, she'd received some unwanted attention that could have landed her in serious trouble if Dylan hadn't intervened. But she couldn't remember the

last time she'd felt more alive. More free. More connected to and capti-
vated by the world around her.

And on that note...

"So all these creatures," she began excitedly, "the entire supernatural
community I learned about as a kid...they're all real?" She felt silly
asking the question, but on the other hand she couldn't help but be
amazed. As a rule, magic was never allowed within the castle—Alwyn
aside—and although she'd grown up reading about 'mythical' creatures
to her heart's content, she and the rest of the kingdom had been led
to believe that most everything had been decimated to the point of ex-
tinction over the course of the rebellions. Magic was little more than a
myth. Her books were little more than fairytales.

But what she saw today...that defied the imagination! And she'd
seen a giant! Had lunch with the fine chap!

"I have no idea what you learned as a child," Dylan responded. "But
after having spent most of my life amongst them, I know for a fact
they'll resent being called *creatures*. Best keep that term to yourself."

Katerina nodded swiftly, but she was on a roll. Her mind was racing
and her eyes were dancing with a million memories she could hardly
dare to believe. "But what about mermaids?" she questioned, rapid-fire.
"If there're such things as hags, *please* tell me there're such things as
mermaids!"

Dylan laughed, clearly unable to stop himself. "How are we actually
having this conversation?"

"And what about werewolves?!" Her eyes widened at the mere
thought. She remembered the pictures from her stories. Giant black
wolves, silhouetted against the shadowy horizon. They were terrifying.
Absolutely terrifying. "You know, it's coming up on a full moon—"

"There are no such things as werewolves." He cast her a sideways
glance and continued cautiously forward. "There are *wolves*—shifters, I
mean. The men we ran into by the wagons, they're from a well-known
pack."

She stopped dead in her tracks, staring up at him in shock. "Are you serious? How do you know that?"

One way or another, it certainly explained his sudden discovery of manners. Discounting that little bit at the end with the knife.

He ran a hand back through his hair, keeping his eyes fixed on the ground. "I've been out here for a while, Kat. You get to know people. You get to know where they're from."

She didn't understand his sudden caginess. The sudden need to avoid her gaze. But, at the moment, her mind was too wrapped up in other matters to really notice. "I can't believe they shift into wolves. I mean, you did say something about shifters, but at the time I hadn't really been paying attention. I was more worried about staying alive. But wolves? That's something I never would've guessed."

His eyes danced with sudden amusement as he turned to look at her for the first time. "Why do you say that?"

"They were huge! The guy in charge had a neck the size of my leg." She shook her head and continued marching through the underbrush. "I assumed they shifted into bison or something."

Dylan threw his head back with a sudden laugh. The same sparkling sound she'd heard when she was swimming. The one that echoed brightly through the trees. She glanced at him from the corner of her eye and found herself star-struck, the same way she'd been the first time they met.

It wasn't something he could hide. And it wasn't something he could fake. Whatever it was about him, it was deep inside his bones. A stunning magnetism that seemed to draw in everyone else around him. An almost otherworldly beauty, as if he'd been kissed by some distant star.

Truth...who are you?

She wanted to ask. She wanted to ask more than anything in the world.

But she didn't. If only because she didn't want to do anything to risk losing that breathtaking smile. She asked another question instead. One that was only slightly less important.

"So... what about mermaids?"

The laughter continued, and without seeming to think about it he reached out to tuck a lock of her fiery red hair behind her ear. "I've never seen a mermaid. Although I would very much like to."

Katerina snorted as they scampered up the side of a ravine and headed into a clearing just beyond. "Yeah, I bet you would. Until she lured you to the edge of the water and pulled you in."

"I'm sure I wouldn't mind."

"Until you drowned?"

"...yeah, until I drowned."

The two of them laughed again, hands in their pockets, kicking up piles of leaves as they made their way through the picturesque meadow. *It really is beautiful*, Katerina thought as she gazed around. *Peaceful.* A little postcard, bordered on all sides by mountain trees.

It was the kind of place where it seemed like nothing bad could ever happen. A tranquil little oasis, hidden from the rest of the tumultuous world. A part of her would happily stay there forever.

Of course, that's when the postcard shattered into a million little pieces.

"Whatever happens next, it's important that you don't scream."

Katerina's head jerked up in surprise as her happy thought bubble popped mid-air. "...what?"

But Dylan was already gone. In a movement almost too fast to follow, he doubled back suddenly and leapt into a grove of trees. There was a violent scuffle, followed by a high-pitched shriek. When he emerged, a moment later, he was dragging someone out by the arm.

What the heck?!

Katerina stumbled back in shock, then let out a forbidden scream.

At a first glance, the girl looked rather wild. There were leaves in her hair, brambles in her clothes, and a thick coating of dirt had painted her from head to toe.

At a second glance, the girl looked rather beautiful. She was about their age, just eighteen or nineteen years old, and had deceptively delicate features considering the ferocity of her scowl. Her eyes were a light hazel that glowed green when they caught the light, and her hair was the exact color of cinnamon, falling in a straight line down to her shoulders.

She was stunning, but oddly frightening at the same time. Like a homicidal doll who'd gotten lost in the woods. A doll who was doing her very best to kick Dylan's ass.

"Let me GO you little worm!" She leapt up with a ferocious kick, but he held her far enough away that it couldn't touch him. "I didn't do ANYTHING!"

In a move that was just as surprising as it was effective she flipped over where she stood, wrenching her arm free in the process. It was a magnificent show of both grace and agility, performed at a blinding speed.

Unfortunately, Dylan caught her again the second she landed. "No, you didn't do anything," he replied, sounding remarkably calm considering the circumstances. "You've just been following us for the last ten miles."

The girl stopped struggling at the same time Katerina's mouth fell open in shock. "Ten miles? And you knew this whole time?!" she cried. "Why didn't you say anything?!"

"I had to be sure she wasn't a spy." Dylan answered her question, but kept his eyes locked on the stranger the whole time. "That she wasn't sent ahead to lead the others. But it's been ten miles. And she hasn't made any intentional tracks."

Okay, how the heck does he KNOW that?! He was talking with me the whole time!

Although her entire nefarious plot had been called into the open, the girl didn't back down for an instant. In fact, she seemed incapable of admitting defeat. "I might just be going the same direction. You don't know!" She tugged at her arm again, literally growling in frustration when it didn't budge. Her second kick failed to land as well so she settled for stomping on Dylan's foot, smearing it with mud.

Katerina didn't understand it. The unwavering spirit. The unshakable defiance that seemed to dictate her every move. It didn't seem to matter that she only came up to Dylan's chin. It didn't seem to matter that she was outnumbered two-to-one and had been caught red-handed.

When Dylan failed to release her, she punched him as hard as she could in the chest...then lifted her head with a vicious glare when he failed to react.

"...coward."

What?!

The initial alarm at being followed had begun to fade, and Katerina was finding herself strangely endeared to the girl. At the very least she deserved to be committed, not imprisoned.

Unfortunately, not everyone shared her generous view.

"Okay." Dylan took a deep breath, visibly reining in his temper. "So are you going to tell me why you've been shadowing us or not?"

He seemed to anticipate what her answer would be. Sure enough, the second he asked the question she took on the expression of a sixth-century martyr. Tilting back her head with an air of righteous indignation worthy of the theater itself.

"Not until you release me and apologize for my so-called capture." She jutted out her chin, matching him glare for glare. "At which point, I'll require some of your cider. Some of us weren't able to rehydrate every time we took a break."

"Unbelievable." Without another word, Dylan tightened his grasp and began dragging her back into the woods, muttering dark profanities under his breath the entire time.

The girl dug in her heels, but was no match against his weight, while Katerina hurried after them with a shout.

"Dylan—you can't *kill* her!"

He never broke his stride. By now, his prisoner was leaving little trenches in her wake. "I'm not going to kill her," he said resolutely. "I'm going to tie her to a tree."

The girl folded her arms across her chest with an evil smirk. "You think that'll stop me?"

Okay, on second thought, she's legitimately crazy.

Katerina stopped in her tracks and watched as Dylan shoved her up against the base of a wide oak. It wasn't until he fished the rope from his pack that she seemed to understand her plight.

"I'm not crazy."

Both Dylan and Katerina looked up warily. They must've been thinking the same exact thing. An almost cartoonish look of conflict washed across the girl's face, as if it was physically paining her to be the first to back down. Then her shoulders wilted and her face cleared with a sudden sigh.

"I'm not crazy," she said again. "I saw you by the wagons, heard that you were heading toward the Black Forest. I thought maybe I could come along."

If it was possible, this made the least amount of sense yet.

"You saw us by the wagons?" Dylan repeated. One look at his face said he wasn't in the mood to play games. "That's funny, I didn't see you."

For whatever reason, the girl blushed. Her hands twitched nervously by her side, and she seemed to be bracing herself for something. "That's because I wasn't exactly feeling like myself."

For a second, the three of them just stood there. Then the girl disappeared.

"Kat—get back!"

Katerina stumbled backwards with a gasp, while Dylan's hand flew to his blade. It took them a second to realize that she hadn't vanished after all, she had merely shrunk in size...

And turned into a goblin?

The tiny creature blinked up at them. Giant ears. Hooked nose. The works. The ropes dropped from Dylan's hand as the goblin-girl did a little curtsey, complete with an apologetic smile.

"The name's Tanya Oberon. Pleased to meet you."

This is...a little too much.

Katerina fell back another step, hand over her heart, while Dylan tried his very best to keep his composure. "You were...you were one of the goblins back at the wagons?"

"I was." The air around the little beast seemed to shimmer, and a second later, the girl, Tanya, was standing back in its place. "I even introduced myself. But this is my true form."

Introduced herself? What does she...

Katerina clapped a hand over her mouth. *SEVEN HELLS! She's the goblin who grabbed Dylan's ass!*

Dylan made the connection at the same time. His lips parted in shock as he stared down at the tiny girl, temporarily speechless. "That was you?!"

She flashed a devilish smirk, and Katerina warmed to her on the spot.

But personal boundaries aside, there was a far more obvious issue that needed to be discussed. The implications of which Katerina was only beginning to understand.

"You're a shifter?" she asked curiously.

Tanya turned to her slowly and nodded. For a moment, the two girls simply stared at one another. Then Tanya's nervous hesitation suddenly made sense.

A shifter that doesn't turn into an animal. A shifter that turns into people instead.

Dylan took a step forward, a completely indecipherable expression on his face. "You're a *shape*-shifter."

Tanya nodded again. Then hung her head.

Katerina pursed her lips. Thinking hard to remember the stories she'd heard as a kid. Shape-shifters. They were the scourge of the shifter world. Regarded with even more disdain than most of the other magical creatures who made up the realm. To shift with no affiliation, no pack, was considered the lowest form of magic. Unfit to even claim the shifter name.

Her eyes flickered up to Dylan, bracing automatically for his censure.

Except Dylan wasn't one to judge. In fact, he looked her up and down with interest before flashing a small smile. "If only we were all so lucky."

It was like popping a balloon. The second he said the words the tension in the little clearing suddenly disappeared, and the unlikely trio was finally able to breathe. No longer were they standing at odds against each other. There was a chance they could even be on the same side.

"So, Tanya Oberon," Dylan inclined his head with an introductory grin, "why is it that you want to come with us to the Black Forest?" As he spoke, he reached into his pack and pulled out a bottle of cider.

Tanya took it with a grateful smile, biting off the cork and gulping down half. A second later, she gulped down the rest.

Katerina and Dylan shared a secret grin.

For a moment, things were looking up. For a moment, it looked as though everyone might actually be getting friendly.

But such things were never meant to last.

She tossed back the empty bottle with a grin, completely oblivious to the disastrous effect of her next words. "Well, to help protect the princess, of course."

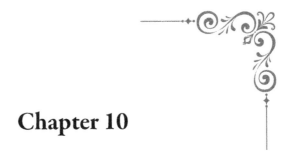

Chapter 10

"WHAT PRINCESS?" DYLAN looked behind him.

Katerina looked up, but not before shooting Tanya an if-looks-could-kill look.

"Her." Tanya clearly didn't notice Katerina's glare.

"I'm not a princess."

At the same time, Dylan said, "She's not the princess."

Though, somehow, Katerina thought he didn't sound very convincing.

Several arguments happened over the course of the next few minutes. A combination of searing accusations, heated denials, vile profanities, and an eventual confession.

"I'm the princess," Katerina said quietly, staring at the ground when she knew there was no denying it any longer.

What resulted was a three-way shouting match, the likes of which the peaceful little clearing had never heard. A showdown for the ages but, strangely enough, when the dust settled it had very little to do with the apologetic shape-shifter. It was between the princess and her reluctant protector.

Dylan hadn't been surprised by the confession. Because he already knew. "I know."

"Why didn't you tell me?!" Katerina shouted as she stormed into the woods. "This whole time, I've been *killing* myself trying to keep it secret! Worrying about it day and night! Living in a constant state of panic! This *whole time*, Dylan, and you already freakin' knew!"

The shape-shifter was wisely keeping her distance, but the princess was in a rage. Without a second thought, she threw down her pack and marched blindly into the woods. She didn't care where she was going. She didn't if she ever found her way back. The only thing she cared about was getting as much space between her and Dylan Aires as possible.

Of course, that didn't stop her from screaming at the top of her lungs.

"You had *no reason*!" she shouted. "*No reason* in the world to keep it to yourself! Other than everything has to be so freakin' mysterious with you. Other than you like to play sick little games—"

"You're mad at *me*?!" One second, he was back in the clearing. The next, he was grabbing her by the arm, yanking her to a sudden stop. "I don't believe it. *You're* mad at me!"

"Why didn't you tell me—"

"Why didn't you tell *me*?!" The space between them grew abruptly quiet. Filled only with the sound of their shallow breathing, their chests heaving up and down. "I'm the one who has a right to be angry here, *Katerina*, not you!"

She flinched when he said her full name. There was a time when she might have wanted to hear him say it. But now, it sounded harsh and unforgiving to her ears. "I told you I'd run away from my family," she mumbled.

"Yes, but you didn't tell me it was the *royal* family," he spat. "That makes a little bit of a difference, don't you think?"

All at once, her rage disappeared. It had been brought about by panic and a misguided sense of betrayal, but it was hypocrisy at its worse. He was right. She should have told him from the start.

Her eyes lowered to the forest floor, but Dylan wasn't the type to let her off the hook so easily. He stood tall and firm in front of her, refusing to budge an inch.

"You didn't think I had a right to know what I was getting in to?" His voice had dropped to that soft, dangerous clip he'd used the night they met at the tavern. The one that sent chills down her spine. "That the people coming after you weren't some disgruntled relatives, but royal soldiers? Soldiers, and knights, and who the heck knows what else?!"

She hung her head as she felt the anger, knew his eyes flashed with rage.

"Maybe it was just that I'm a commoner." His face hardened in disgust. "What's the life of one ranger? We're all expendable to you people—"

"That's not true!" A pair of tears flew down her face as she finally lifted her head to face him. "You have to know that's not true!"

He grew unexpectedly gentle. His sky-blue eyes softened, and every hint of anger vanished from his handsome face as he stared at the wetness on her cheeks. "Then why didn't you tell me?" he asked softly, bending down to hold her gaze. "You had so many chances..."

Yes, she had. And she'd almost taken them, every single time. By this point, Katerina couldn't even remember how many times she'd almost spilled her secret. When they were trekking through the woods each afternoon. When they were packing up the tent each morning. When they were sitting beside the evening fire, telling stories and staring up at the stars. She'd almost told him every single time. But something hadn't let her. Something held her back.

"I didn't want you to leave me."

The interrogation came to an abrupt stop as the quiet words were whispered between them. She hadn't realized them herself until she'd said them out loud, and they were certainly the last thing he'd expected to hear. He pulled back a few inches, searching her face for the truth.

"You thought that would happen?" he finally asked. "You actually thought I'd leave you?"

She bit down on her lip, refusing to let herself cry. "You did it once. Why wouldn't you do it again? When the stakes were so much higher? When there was a chance you could be killed? And to do it for—"

She broke off suddenly, refusing to let herself say anymore. Things were finally honest between them, but she'd come dangerously close to the edge of a terrible truth. A truth that had been haunting her every day since she'd left the castle.

Another tear slipped down her cheek, but a warm hand wiped it away. Tilting her face until she was staring into a pair of staggering eyes. "To do it for...what?"

For a fleeting moment, all she could do was stare. The second she said the words, it would be over. The strange understanding that had sprung up between them would be gone, and she'd be very lucky if he didn't decide to leave with it. Then the moment passed, and she pulled in a breath. "To do it for a princess."

Never before had she hated the position she held until that very moment. Never before had she been ashamed of her birth, repulsed by her own legacy. But it was true. She had seen firsthand the way the 'other half' lived. In poverty. In fear. In the knowledge that they were perceived as less by those who were supposed to protect and lead them. And she knew firsthand, after spending her entire life in the castle, that they were absolutely right.

Her family were the oppressors. These people were the oppressed. That's all there was to it.

"Before I left the castle, I didn't know..." She trailed off, lifting her eyes to the horizon as the faces of those she'd met on her travels flashed before her eyes. Finally, when the silence could go on no longer, she simply said, "If I was in your place, I wouldn't want to help someone like me."

For the second time, they lapsed into silence. It seemed an odd place to be so...at odds. The birds were chirping in the trees above them.

The afternoon breeze was rustling through their hair. If it wasn't for what they were discussing, it would have made a lovely portrait.

Then Dylan's quiet voice brought the picture back to life. "And what gives me the right to judge?"

Katerina looked up in shock. Convinced she hadn't heard him correctly. Convinced he'd meant to say goodbye instead. "I'm... excuse me, sorry?"

"Did you turn your father against his own realm? Did you enforce his laws? Write his policies?" His eyes gentled as they stared down into hers. "Did you fight in his rebellions?"

She couldn't speak. Couldn't breathe. She merely shook her head.

He bowed his head with the softest sigh before looking back up with a sad smile. "You cannot judge a person based on where they're from. You cannot hold a person responsible for the sins of their family. If there's anyone who knows that, it's me."

She didn't completely understand what he was saying. She certainly didn't understand how it connected to him.

But at least one thing had been made perfectly clear.

She was forgiven.

According to Dylan, there was nothing to forgive.

The wind danced her hair around in a fiery cloud as she gave him a tentative smile. "So you've known from the very beginning, huh? Am I that obvious? Or did the fairies tell you?"

He laughed softly, combing back his dark hair. "They didn't have to tell me. I've always known. From the minute I laid eyes on you."

Katerina nodded, then froze. Her heart quickened as she asked the final question. "Is it why you left?"

He was quiet for a moment, then his eyes danced with a twinkling smile. "It's why I came back."

IT SAID A LOT ABOUT the weight of Katerina's confession that the two most cautious people in the world had left their self-proclaimed stalker unsupervised. Little flutters of nerves started beating away in the princess' stomach as she realized that she'd also left her pack. But the moment they returned to the clearing, all their fears were put to rest.

While she had clearly been eavesdropping, Tanya had also been busy. The tent was pitched between two tall trees bordering the clearing, exactly where Dylan would have pitched it himself. A blazing fire was already waiting to greet them, and a caldron full of what smelled like the world's most delicious stew hung bubbling over the flames.

She looked up immediately when they came into view, her silky hair swinging lightly atop her shoulders. "Oh, hello there! While you two were screaming at each other, I decided to make myself useful by pilfering through Her Highness's pack. Found some food inside. Hope you don't mind."

For a second, Katerina was worried very much that Dylan *would* mind. He didn't exactly take kindly to strangers, and was even less inclined to share his things. But his eyes flickered over the little camp before warming with a gracious smile.

"Not at all. What's ours is yours."

It was the stew. He smelled the stew.

Tanya pushed immediately to her feet, looking from one to the other as she perched on the tips of her toes. "Do you really mean that? I can stay?"

Dylan looked her up and down before turning to Katerina. "What do you think, Kat? Could we use one more misfit?"

At this point, Katerina fervently believed they could use all the help they could get. And if that help happened to come in the form of an ass-grabbing, back-talking, princess-stalking, shape-shifting misfit...well, so much the better. "Absolutely." She settled down onto the log without a second thought, patting the spot beside her with a grin. "Welcome to our crew."

It was perhaps the last thing that any of them had expected to happen when they woke up that morning, but despite their violent introduction, by the time they sat down around the fire, passing out bowls of stew, it was clear to see the trio had all the makings to become fast friends.

The initial introductions and standard pleasantries soon gave way to hilarious stories and the sort of bawdy jokes that would never have been allowed at the castle. The initial social boundaries soon broke down with a familiarity and natural sort of ease that spoke to years of acquaintance, not a simple shared meal over the flames of a campfire.

Tanya Oberon was a bright, vivacious girl with a searing wit and a caustic sense of humor that left even the impassive Dylan shaking with silent laughter. Blessed with both beauty and brains, the whole world should have opened its doors, but alas, such a thing was never meant to be. For no matter how high she was able to rise on her own merits, she was tethered down by a social prejudice she was unable to shake. The stigma of a shape-shifter was a shadow that followed her wherever she went. Closing those doors. Vanishing those opportunities. Turning that bright, vivacious girl into an outsider. A perpetual nomad, doomed to travel from place to place. Never settling. Never assimilating. Never able to find a place where she could truly belong.

It hadn't dampened her, exactly. It had roughly the same effect that it had on Dylan.

Instilling caution instead of trust. Experience instead of optimism. Creating walls where perhaps none had existed before. Her past, specifically, was a subject she seemed determined to avoid. Where she had come from and how she had joined up with the shifter caravan remained a mystery. What *was* made clear, was how eager she was to leave.

"—which is when I realized not only that we weren't going for ice cream after all, but also that The Sultry Scullion was, in fact, a brothel." She bit her lower lip, staring down contemplatively into her stew. "In hindsight, the name probably should have cued me in..."

Katerina's sides hurt from both laughing and trying to hold the laughter in. She had never in her life met such a paradox. The girl was her own worst enemy, and her own best friend. Either way, she was a force to be reckoned with.

"Don't feel bad." Dylan pulled out a silver flask and took a swig of whiskey. The flask was then passed around the fire. "I once spent three days at a Bedouin solstice party before realizing I had unwittingly married the chief's daughter on the first night."

The girls raised their eyebrows at the same time, and he hastily clarified.

"...I had it annulled."

Tanya burst out laughing, helping herself to more whiskey, but Katerina felt the strong need to contribute something. Over the course of the night it had become clear that, while the unlikely trio was approximately the same age, they had vastly different levels of experience. Both Tanya and Dylan had been on their own since childhood. Travelling the world. Drifting from adventure to adventure. Getting into the kinds of mischief that one could hardly believe.

But Katerina? The high princess of all the land? She had scarcely been outside the walls of the castle. Until a few weeks ago she'd had yet to leave the kingdom, and although the courtiers and dignitaries who visited the court were from all over the world they lived in their own bubbles of luxurious isolation. Never would they find themselves in a goblin brothel. Never would they dare travel to the badlands, let alone be savvy enough to come back and tell the tale.

As if sensing her exclusion, Tanya provided a gracious opening.

"What about you, princess? I'm sure you have some stories to tell."

The others turned to her expectedly and Katerina froze on the spot. The whiskey was already making her a little light-headed, and it certainly didn't help to be trapped in the piercing gaze of two sets of eyes. She opened her mouth once or twice, but came up blank. A sort of panic set over her, and in the end she blurted out the first thing that came into her mind.

"I snuck down to the kitchens one time when I was supposed to be at dance class." Two blank faces stared back at her across the fire, and she hurried to defend her work. "It was in the servants' hall. A place Kailas and I were most definitely *not* supposed to go."

It had felt quite rebellious at the time. But when she said it out loud...

A profound silence followed this remark. One made all the worse by the looks of restrained amusement on Dylan's and Tanya's faces. They looked quickly down at the fire, hiding their smile but, fortunately, they didn't make her wait too long.

The impromptu confession brought up a rather serious subject. One the trio had been strategically dancing around the entire time.

"I won't ask why exactly you're on the run," Tanya began slowly. "I saw the beacon, just like everyone else. I'm assuming it has something to do with the death of your father."

It was a gracious out, but a clear opening at the same time. An open invitation for the princess to tell them whatever she so desired. And while Katerina would rather walk through fire than relive what had happened that terrible night, she felt as though she had to tell. Dylan was right: The two of them were risking their lives to protect her. They deserved to know why.

"My father didn't just die...he was murdered," she said softly. "Stabbed through the heart while he slept. One of the knights came to tell me about it. He helped get me out of the castle."

The unspoken question hung between them. Like a dark cloud hovering in the air. Neither of the others could bring themselves to ask, and Katerina wouldn't make them.

After a moment of silence, she answered it herself.

"It was my brother."

There was a soft gasp as Tanya clapped her hands over her mouth. Even Dylan couldn't fully hide his surprise. His blue eyes widened in the dark before dropping down to the flames. Shining with sympathy. Lost in thought. Flickering with the dancing flames.

"He wants me dead. I'm the eldest. I'm next in line. Without me..."

It was quiet for a long time. The pleasant buzz created by the whiskey had suddenly sobered, and the cheerful evening had abruptly chilled in the breeze. Katerina looked from one to the other, both of whom were avoiding her gaze. She felt strangely relieved to have gotten the secret off her chest, but she wondered if they would have rather been kept in the dark. If they regretted bringing up the question and learning the terrible truth. It was a heavy burden. One that came with a price.

Finally, when the silence could go on no longer, Tanya lifted her head. "So where does that leave us?" she asked quietly.

Katerina's heart literally warmed in her chest. Her eyes welled up as she stared across the fire at the strange girl. A girl who was willing to help her no matter what stakes were leveled against them. A girl who was willing to risk her very life for someone she hardly knew.

"Are you...are you serious?" She hardly dared to ask the question, at the risk of changing the answer. "You're willing to stay?"

Tanya met her gaze for a split second before shrugging it off with a signature grin. "It's better than spending my time at the height of a trash can, staring at people's knees."

Katerina let out a gasp of breathless laughter before turning to Dylan. He, too, met her eyes and a knowing look passed between them.

The same question she'd asked Tanya died on the tip of her tongue. There was no need to ask it again. She already knew the answer.

She asked another instead. Effectively placing her life in his steady hands.

"So where *does* this leave us?"

It was one thing to be on the run from her brother and his minions. Hiding in the woods from contingents of royal guards and military servicemen. Both of whom were predictable. Both of whom would find it completely impossible to blend in. It was another thing entirely if they were dancing around the edge of a civil war. A covert, one-sided war. The kind that used mercenaries and assassins. The kind that pitted prince against princess. Brother against sister. Locked in a deadly race to the throne.

Dylan thought about it a long time, frowning slightly as he stared into the flames. "I think it says a lot that your brother hasn't put a bounty on your head," he finally answered. "If people knew the truth, he's afraid they'd rally around you to help you take back the throne. He's obviously hoping he can have you killed before that's an option."

A few weeks ago, those words would have shocked Katerina to the core. As it stood, she absorbed them silently and focused on the next step of the plan. "So, then, why don't I just tell people who I am?"

Dylan and Tanya exchanged a quick look before answering.

"Because your brother is underestimating the realm's goodwill towards the entire royal family," he said almost apologetically. "You tell people in these parts you descend from the Damaris bloodline, and they'll likely find your body in a ditch the next morning."

"No offense," Tanya added hastily.

Katerina nodded, feeling a bit dazed. "...of course not."

Only Dylan remained unaffected. But he wasn't the type to shy away from hard truths. "We'll tell people in time, but they will be the *right* people," he said quietly, almost to himself, planning as he went. "And only at a time when you're safe."

It sounded practical enough. Especially considering Dylan was the one saying it. But it begged the obvious question.

A question Tanya had no problem pointing out. "And how exactly is she going to *get* safe?"

A little shiver rocketed up Katerina's spine, and she wrapped her cloak tighter around herself. Tanya was right. Alone in the middle of the woods, so outnumbered and exposed it seemed almost impossible. How could she fight a war without an army? How could she take the throne with two people? How could she even manage to stay alive, if these were the odds stacked against them?

It wasn't like they could hide out in the wilderness forever. And it wasn't like a princess on the run was an easy secret to keep. Tanya had guessed who she was simply because she recognized her face from royal portraits and decrees. It was only a matter of time before someone else did the same thing. Someone who wasn't as sympathetic to her cause.

So the question remained: What the heck were they going to do?

"I don't know," Dylan murmured, staring off into the shadowy trees. "But I know someone who can help..."

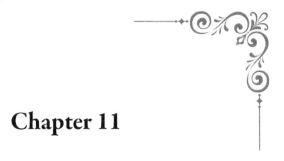

Chapter 11

THE MORE TIME KATERINA spent in the world outside the castle, the more she realized how inter-connected it really was. Over the next few days of travelling, there wasn't a town or village that either Dylan or Tanya hadn't been to personally. There wasn't a situation or creature they hadn't dealt with before. There wasn't a single barman they didn't know by name.

By the time they ended up in Lakewood, the town for which they'd been aiming, Katerina had developed a whole new level of respect for her travelling companions. What was more, they'd developed a whole new level of respect for each other.

"Dylan, if you don't slow down, I'm going to stab you in the back with a tent peg."

Respect. Friendship was still a ways off.

The ranger cast a long-suffering look behind him, but slowed his pace as they made their way out of the forest and onto a bluff that overlooked the town. It was here that the trio came to a simultaneous stop, looking down with a bit of apprehension as they considered what was to come.

Dylan had been deliberately vague about the 'old friend' they were travelling to meet. The one who would supposedly help them on their journey. Whatever it was he was keeping to himself, the girls didn't know. But one way or another, they were in no position to be refusing help.

"How do you know he'll be here?" Katerina asked curiously. "You guys keep in touch?"

"Not much," Dylan replied evasively, shifting his weight as he gazed out over the town. "But Lakewood's hosting the Festival of Woodland Lights. He'll be here. And he won't be hard to find."

The girls exchanged a quick look. Won't be hard to find? What did that mean?

"Come on." Dylan seemed eager to end the conversation before it could really get off the ground. "It's coming up on mid-day. With any luck, he's still in bed. And mostly sober..."

Another look. This time it was paired with a grin.

Katerina's mind bubbled with a million questions, but she held her tongue. Even Tanya, who had no filter whatsoever, had the sense to keep quiet. Instead, the three of them started heading down the mountain. Bracing for whatever mischief the day had in store...

MAGICAL HOLIDAYS WERE never celebrated in the castle. As such, Katerina had never even heard of the Festival of Woodland Lights. But walking through the town, it quickly became clear what Dylan meant when he said his friend would be there. There wasn't a man in the realm who wasn't.

The purpose of the festival was to celebrate the spirits of the forest along with the coming of the new celestial year. To get into the festive mood, the store fronts were strung with garlands of white flowers. Giant vats of nectar and ambrosia cast a heavenly aroma over the streets. Musicians armed with fiddles and lutes were walking through the crowd, and the festival-goers had painted their faces green in order to honor the spirit of the trees...

...which meant that all the wood nymphs had come out to play.

Never before had the princess seen so many beautiful women in one place. And beautiful didn't begin to cover it. She had long ago read that nymphs were famed for their beauty, but the writing in the castle library hardly did them justice.

They were like angels. Waif-like, woodsy angels that floated along down the street. Dresses of gauzy silk. Clouds of white hair that fell down to their waists. Eyes so bright, they made everything around them dim in comparison. They moved in little clusters. Pausing every now and then to buy another flowery adornment for their long hair. Casting occasional glances in mirrors and store-front windows to admire their flawless reflections. Shooting bewitching smiles at the gaggles of men that followed in their wake—openly salivating as they tried to remember how to speak.

Katerina raised her eyebrows as one of them blew a playful kiss at Dylan, shaking back a wave of silky white-blonde hair. Her friends were quick to pick up on the chase—shooting curious glances at the rugged ranger as they giggled quietly and whispered behind their hands.

Obvious, much?

He blushed faintly, but did nothing to encourage them. He merely flashed a polite smile as he and the girls walked past. Unfortunately, that did nothing to stop the giggling. Nor did it stop Tanya from taking great delight in the entire exchange. Her face lit up with mischief as she ostentatiously elbowed him in the ribs, raising her voice for everyone to hear.

"What's that?" She cupped a hand around her ear with a theatric frown. "You just got out of a serious relationship, and you're looking for someone special to help you rebuild?"

He looked down with a start, paling to the color of sour milk as he lowered his voice to a frantic hiss. "What the heck are you doing?"

"Well, I know you're shy, sweetie, but you've just got to get past it." She patted him sympathetically on the shoulder, staying carefully out of reach of his blade. "Nobody here is going to judge. We all just want what's best for you."

He grabbed the back of her coat and dragged her along at a faster pace, ignoring the chorus of snickering laughter that followed in their wake.

"Okay, level with me...do you really have a friend here, or did you just want to find a nymph?"

Even Katerina had to smile at that one, but Dylan shot the shifter a look that promised certain death the second they were out of the public eye. Sensing trouble, the princess intercepted the look and pulled them both to a stop as they reached a fountain in the center of the town square.

"You, hand over the dagger. You, keep the colorful commentary to yourself unless you want to get killed." She cast each one a stern look of warning before glancing back at the bustling crowd. "Let's just find this friend of yours and get the bloody heck out of here." She cast Dylan a sideways glance. "The less time we spend out in the open, the better."

For all our sakes.

"Fine." Tanya rolled her eyes, but abandoned her teasing and got down to business. "You said this guy wouldn't be hard to find. What did you mean?"

With a quiet sigh, Dylan slipped his knife back into its sheath.

"That's easy." His eyes drifted briefly around the square before zeroing in on a specific target. "Just look for the fanciest hotel..."

OVER THE COURSE OF the last few weeks, Katerina had seen Dylan in a variety of different circumstances. She'd seen him tired, and charming, and defensive, and even adorably upbeat. She'd never once seen him nervous. Not until that very moment.

"Okay, Dylan, what the heck happened with this guy?? Did you accidentally kill his dog? Or purposely?"

They were standing in front of the door to the best room in the best tavern in the entire town. The proprietor had confirmed the identity of his guest, after a significant bribe, and after locating the correct room all that was left to do was knock on the door.

Except that Dylan couldn't seem to raise his hand.

He shot Katerina a quick glance, as if she wasn't too far off the mark, before forcing a casual smile onto his face. "No, it's...it's going to be fine." He lifted his hand, then paused again, staring at the door like it had burst into flames. An almost sickly expression swept over him and he muttered the words again, saying them only to himself. "It's going to be fine."

After taking a deep breath, he knocked three times on the door.

By now, even the girls were a bit nervous as to what was waiting on the other side. Was the man going to be horrifically disfigured? Had Dylan accidentally set the guy on fire? Burned off an arm? They listened breathlessly as the silence gave way to a faint shuffling, then the sound of light footsteps making their way to the door. By the time it pulled open, they had mentally prepared themselves for anything and everything.

Except for the exquisite nymph who stood in the doorway.

"Yes?"

Everything about her was perfect. From her pearly smile, to her sparkling eyes, to the silky hair that billowed in waves down her bare back. Both Katerina and Tanya exchanged a quick look of confusion, but Dylan just rolled his eyes with a quiet sigh.

"I'm looking for Cass."

She vanished without another word, closing the door behind her. When it opened again a moment later, there was another nymph. She was even more beautiful than the first. And if it was possible, she was wearing even less clothing. Just a tiny slip that stopped an inch below her thighs.

"Good morning." Her face melted into a welcoming smile as she made a sleepy effort to smooth down her sex-tousled hair. "Are you here with the food?"

Katerina smothered a grin as Tanya bit down on her lip to keep from laughing. Dylan, however, looked almost physically sick as he forced a tight smile.

"Nope. Not here with the food. I'm looking for Cass. Is he here?"

She glanced behind her, gaze resting briefly on the bed, before she turned around with a mischievous giggle. "He's still sleeping. I'm afraid we're all a little worn out."

Dylan's smile tightened into a grimace. "I'll bet. The thing is, I really need to speak with him—"

The door closed again. Mid-sentence. Right in his face. He stared at it a moment, then took a step back, his hands balling into fists as his teeth ground together.

"It had to be nymphs..."

"We should have intercepted their room service." Tanya stepped forward with a grin, raising her hand to knock on the door. "Why don't you let me try this time?"

Dylan took a step back as the air around her seemed to shimmer. By the time her fist came down on the wood she was no longer a young girl, but had taken the shape of a burly village constable. She had the mustache, the badge, everything down to the authoritative scowl.

A scowl that was only slightly ruined when she gave her friends an impish wink.

The door was pulled open by yet a third nymph, but this one stepped back in surprise when she saw the officer standing in front of her. Her eyes widened and she hurried to slip on a robe.

"Can I help you, Constable?"

Tanya didn't waste any time. And she didn't pull any punches. "This is the third time my associates and I have knocked on this door, and let me assure you there will not be a fourth. We're looking for a man named Cass. Now either you send him out in the next thirty seconds, or I'm going to cite you for obstruction of justice."

The girl melted away so fast, Katerina could have sworn she vanished on the spot. The three of them waited in tense silence, wondering if their plan had worked, but only a few seconds later the door pulled open again and a beautiful man walked outside.

Holy bloomin' cow!

Katerina said 'man' because she didn't know what else to call him. And she said 'beautiful' even though the word fell utterly short. It was like the guy walked straight out of a fairytale.

He was pure grace. There was no other way to describe him. An ethereal, radiant sort of grace that seemed to shine a little brighter than everything in the world around it. He was as tall as Dylan, and just as strong. But while one man was all dark—tan skin, chocolate hair—the other was all light. Fair skin. A silver tunic. White-blond hair that fell to his shoulders. The only thing that differed were his eyes. He had dark, rich eyes. Eyes that shone so bright, they leapt right off his face.

Right now, those enchanting eyes were resting curiously on Constable Tanya.

"My apologies," he said courteously. "What seems to be the..."

He trailed off a second later, staring in absolute shock.

Katerina felt Dylan stiffen beside her, and sure enough it only took a moment for that lovely face to tighten with unspeakable rage.

"...*you.*"

Dylan held up his hands, trying his very best to project an air of rational calm.

"Now, just hold on a second. Let's not do anything we'll both—"

A sudden punch caught him right in the face.

"—regret."

A river of blood streamed from his nose as he cupped his face in his hand. The other was still raised in supplication, though he didn't seem to expect much of a reprieve.

"Cass, I didn't come here to—"

Another punch. This one was even harder than the first.

"—fight."

Dylan staggered back a step, this time blinking away a stream of blood that was pouring from a cut above his eye. His face tightened with pain as he lifted his free hand like a shield.

"Seven hells, man! Will you just let me—"

A third punch. This one threatened to finish him completely.

"—talk?!"

The nymphs scattered to the four winds, while Katerina and Tanya stood there in absolute shock. They hadn't exactly been expecting a warm welcome, but they certainly hadn't been expecting a blow-out either. That being said, it wasn't like either one of them was particularly inclined to jump in. Not only was it all a bit out of their league, but it sounded like Dylan certainly had it coming. And there wasn't a force in the world that would get them to stand in the way of those fists.

There was a savage cry as Cass lifted Dylan straight off his feet and slammed him into the adjacent wall, dangling him a foot above the floor.

"You dare to come here?!" he cried, smashing his head against the stone. "You dare to look me in the face?! After what you've done!"

Yep, certainly had it coming.

Cass bashed him into the wall once more, his blonde hair falling to reveal the tips of his pointed ears. It was only then Katerina realized what he was. Realized that he wasn't a man at all. Realized why he looked like the ancient prince from all of her storybooks come to life.

He's a fae.

She sucked in a gasp of surprise, staring in fascination. Completely ignoring the fact that her new best friend was slowly getting beaten to a pulp against a hotel wall.

I can't believe it! Right here in the flesh!

Dylan was slightly less enchanted. He was making no attempt to defend himself, but that did nothing to temper the fae's rage. It wasn't until an *actual* constable rounded the corner that the four of them slipped inside the hotel room, closing the door with a hasty *click*.

The second that he was free Dylan fell to his knees, panting, and bleeding freely onto the floor. Tanya melted quickly back to her actual shape, looking pale, while Katerina stared at Cass with equal parts terror and fascination. A childish part of her hoped he would get past his murderous vendetta quickly. Then maybe he'd let her touch his ears...

"Well, now that *that's* out of the way," Dylan began as he pushed painfully to his feet, gesturing from one person to the next, "I believe introductions are in order. Cass, this is Tanya and Katerina. Girls, this is my oldest friend, Cassiel."

All four of them froze perfectly still, looking from one to the other. *What the heck are we supposed to do? Shake hands?*

Luckily, though he might have been about two seconds away from committing a daylight homicide, the fae still seemed to have some manners. He tore his murderous eyes away from Dylan, wiped the blood off his knuckles, and offered a polite hand to each of the women in turn. "A pleasure to meet you," he said softly.

The girls blinked, then hastened to comply.

"Pleasure's all mine."

"Yeah, it's...it's really nice to meet you."

The three of them shook quickly, giving each other a cursory glance before turning back to the fourth member of their party, who was still bleeding a small ocean onto the floor. At this point, exsanguination was an actual risk, but you'd never have known it from his face. Now that the savage beating was over, he seemed to think the little reunion was going brilliantly.

"There—see?" Dylan flashed them all a beaming smile. "No reason we can't all get along."

The girls stared at him in disbelief, while Cassiel gave him an icy glare.

"What do you want, Dylan?" he asked coldly.

A bloody good question. Given the bad blood that was literally stain-ing the ground between them, what could Dylan possibly expect to come of the surprise visit?

As it turned out, his request was as simple as it was disarming.

"I want to buy you a drink."

TEN MINUTES LATER THE four of them were circled around a booth in a local tavern, sitting in an almost comically uncomfortable si-lence. The ranger, the fae, the shifter, and the princess. Never was there such an unlikely gathering, and what a priceless picture they made.

Dylan had yet to stop bleeding, Cassiel was glaring a hole into the table, Tanya was chewing anxiously on her lip, and Katerina was so ner-vous she was having some kind of heart palpitations.

It wasn't until a full minute had passed that Cassiel looked up with a glare.

"So where's the flippin' drink?"

Dylan jumped in surprise, as if he'd been thinking about something else, before pulling a handful of bronze coins out of his pocket and laying them quickly upon the table. "Right. Get yourself whatever you want."

Three pairs of eyes shot down to the coins, each more baffled than the last, then back up to Dylan. Tanya kicked him under the table for good measure.

"Are you serious?" Cassiel asked in disgust. "This is your grand ges-ture?"

"What do you expect?" Dylan shot back. "It looks like a carriage ran over my face."

The two men shared an indecipherable look, but unless Katerina was mistaken she could have sworn there was a hint of a grin beneath it. A second later, Cassiel pushed to his feet with a frustrated sigh, leaving the money behind as he headed off to the bar. The trio stared after him for a moment before Tanya leapt up as well, hurrying after him.

"I'm going to help."

The second it was just Katerina and Dylan, the mood at the table relaxed significantly. It relaxed to the point where she smacked him in the chest before pelting him with peanuts.

"What the *heck* is going on?!" she demanded, lobbing one after another. "You bring us to a festival of lusty nymphs, just to get your butt kicked by the one person in the world you call a *friend*?!"

"Hey!" He grabbed her wrists with a bloody grin, putting an end to the attack. "I have a plan, all right? It's not like we're going into this blind."

She yanked herself free, shaking her head with a reluctant smile. "And that plan is to let the one person you think can help us beat you to a pulp?"

"Yeah, that's the way it starts."

There was a beat of silence.

"And how does it end?"

He wiped his face clean with the hem of his shirt, helping himself to a peanut in the process.

"It ends different than that."

Seven hells! This man is exasperating.

Resigned that it was the only answer she was going to get Katerina leaned back against the cracked leather, staring curiously towards the bar. As much as he seemed to hate Dylan, Cassiel didn't seemed to have any problem with the rest of them. He and Tanya were talking quietly as they waited for drinks, lighting up with the occasional smile whenever something amusing was said.

"So, who is he, anyway?" Katerina asked. "This friend of yours?"

Dylan followed her gaze with a thoughtful expression on his face. Despite having taken a brutal beating, there wasn't an ounce of malice as he stared at the fae. Just a kind of brotherly affection and nostalgia

Katerina didn't completely understand. "Cassiel is one of the High Born."

The surprises just kept coming.

The fae didn't have royalty, but if they did Cassiel would have been in their inner circle. It was even more shocking because, of the thousands of fae that had died in the rebellions, none of the High Born were said to have survived. That being said, the princess was quickly coming to discover that news of the royal army's stunning victories had been greatly exaggerated.

That's all well and good, but why in the world would he ever help me?

Dylan read her thoughts as easily as if she'd spoken them aloud.

"Believe it or not, he actually has a strong moral compass—buried beneath all the bitterness and resentment. A sense of honor." Dylan gave his friend another fond look. "A frightened girl on the run? The legitimate heir to the throne being hunted down by assassins? He won't be able to walk away from something like that."

Katerina's eyebrows shot up in surprise. "So we're going to tell him the truth? That I'm the princess?"

"We're going to have to," Dylan replied practically. "You can't lie to a fae. They'll always know." He glanced towards the bar again before kicking back in his chair. "Besides, Cass is just like every other High Born exiled by your father's rule. He's drunk, and bored, and restless like you wouldn't believe. We can use that."

As if on cue Tanya and Cassiel returned, their arms laden down with drinks. They doled them out around the table before sliding into the booth, smelling of whiskey and looking significantly more relaxed than when they'd left.

"Looks like you started without us," Dylan said with a smile.

Cassiel's eyes flashed up and Katerina braced for another punch but, much to her surprise, the smile was returned. "You've made some charming friends since the last time we met. Do they simply not know you yet, or have you paid them off?"

Dylan took the insult in stride, downing a shot of whisky with a grin. "You'll soon learn that Cass has a delightful sense of humor—just one of his endearing qualities. Second only to that inflated sense of self."

The two girls stiffened but the fae lifted his drink to Dylan's, clinking the glass.

"Cheers."

It was the strangest reconciliation Katerina had ever seen, but it couldn't have been more welcome all around. Together, the four of them downed their whiskey and reached for another. It went down as smoothly as the first, and before long they were starting on their third.

The liquor did the trick. Loosening their tongues and lowering their defenses all at once. It didn't take long for the ice to break and the conversations to begin. It wasn't easy at first, but it did get considerably easier the more they drank. Katerina suspected this was why Dylan suggested a bar.

"So it looked like you were enjoying the festival," Tanya began slyly, shooting the fae a sideways grin as she downed her fourth drink. "I'm sorry if we interrupted..."

"This year wasn't half bad." Cassiel leaned back in his chair, stretching his long legs beneath the table. "It was nothing compared to the summer of forty-two, but—"

"Wait. The summer of forty-two?" Katerina frowned in confusion before glancing at Dylan for help. "But that was almost half a century ago."

Dylan tipped back his drink with a grin. "The fae don't age the way the rest of us do. Cass is about a hundred years old."

Katerina's mouth fell open in shock. He didn't look more than twenty. It could have been an awkward moment, but Cassiel simply offered her a lovely smile. "Eighty of those years were good...then I met Dylan."

The ranger leaned forward with a hopeful smile.

"...and they got great?"

Even Cassiel had to laugh at that one. Albeit, rather reluctantly. The mood at the table lightened even more as the conversation and drinks continued flowing, and it wasn't that long before the better part of an hour had passed. They ordered food, ordered more drinks, and another hour passed by after that. Not long after, they finally came around to the inevitable question.

"So what are you doing here, Dylan?" Cassiel's dark eyes landed on him curiously, taking in every detail. "What kind of trouble have you landed yourself in this time?"

Dylan's eyes flashed instinctively to Katerina before he set his drink down with a deliberate smile. "Believe it or not, it isn't me this time. It's her."

Cassiel followed his gaze, landing on Katerina with a touch of surprise.

Despite the lively conversation, the fae and the princess hadn't talked directly much. Katerina couldn't look at him without feeling incredibly intimidated and shy, and Cassiel wasn't one to force his company. But all that seemed to fall away as they studied each other for the first time.

"You look familiar," he murmured, almost to himself. His dark eyes took on a faraway look as he tried to place it. "I feel like we've met before."

Katerina shifted nervously in her chair, glancing again at Dylan. She was fairly certain that if this beautiful man had stepped anywhere near the castle, she would have remembered. But his age made that another matter entirely. He could have very easily visited the castle when she was only a child, and she would never have known.

"You haven't met her," Dylan said softly. "But I believe you met her mother. Adelaide."

It was hard to tell who was more surprised—the princess or the fae. Both stared at Dylan in complete shock before turning back to each other. Pale as a ghost. At a loss for words. It was quiet for only a fleeting moment, then Cassiel pushed to his feet in a single, fluid movement.

"You've brought me here to help put a Damaris on the throne?" As frightening as they'd seen him, it was nothing compared to how he was now. "You must be out of your bloody mind."

Without another word, he stormed out of the tavern. Leaving them all behind.

They stared after him for a moment, still frozen with shock, before Katerina folded her arms across her chest and shot Dylan a withering glare.

"And was *that* part of the plan?"

A cluster of coins rained down on the table as the three of them bolted outside and into the busy street. The festival was still in full swing, but it only took a second to spot Cassiel striding swiftly through the crowd. Try as he might to blend in, the guy was hard to miss.

"Hey!" Dylan sprinted after him, Katerina and Tanya hot on his tail. "Come on, man, don't just walk away!" Still nothing. The three of them ran faster. "Will you hold on for one da—"

His voice choked off with a sudden gasp as Cassiel spun around at the last second and yanked him into an alley. The girls skidded to a stop on the slick cobblestones a moment later, panting, and watching with wide eyes as the two men faced off.

"A *Damaris*, Dylan?" Cassiel was the first to speak, shoving his friend hard in the chest to make his point. "Katerina *Damaris*—that's who this is?"

The princess shrank back against the wall, suddenly jealous of Tanya's ability to change shape at will. Right now, she'd give anything to have a different face. To have a different name.

Dylan held up his hands, purposely slowing down the building momentum. "She's not what you think. Trust me, I thought the same thing when she first sought me out, but I was wrong—"

"And why exactly did she seek *you* out?" Cassiel's voice took on a strange tone, layered with a context Katerina didn't understand. "Did you ever stop to think about that?"

For a split second, Dylan actually paused. Then he shook his head firmly, refusing to acknowledge whatever implication had been silently made. "The fairies sent her."

That got Cassiel's attention.

He stopped pacing at once, turning to Dylan with honest surprise. His dark eyes dilated with impossible intensity as they took in every inch of the ranger's face, before he slowly turned to the pale-faced, fire-haired girl standing by his side.

"The fairies," he repeated softly, still breathing hard but calming down. "Marigold and—"

"—and Nixie and Beck," Katerina finished quickly, anxious to prove the validity of her claim. "They found me passed out in the woods after... well... it's kind of a long story."

Cassiel's face hardened to beautiful stone. "Summarize."

The word sent chills down her back, and she glanced at Dylan for confirmation. He nodded his head a fraction of an inch and she took a deep breath, bracing once again to tell her story.

"My brother Kailas killed the king." She didn't know why she was calling him the king instead of her father. "He tried to kill me, too, as I'm the next in line for the throne, but I was snuck out of the castle by those I trust. They chased me through the woods, but I managed to make it to the edge of the kingdom before passing out. When I woke up, I met Marigold and the others. They nursed me back to health for a day, then gave me Dylan's name. We've been running ever since."

It was certainly the quick version—missing several key details. But he asked for a summary.

The little alley fell silent as all those gathered absorbed the enormity of those words. Here they were, just four people standing in the middle of a woodland festival, but they happened to be the only four people alive who knew the crown prince had committed high treason.

Unfortunately, that didn't prove enough of a selling point for the fae.

"And why should I care?" He didn't ask the question of Katerina, but of Dylan. Angry as he was, he wouldn't antagonize a young woman about the death of her kin. "Tell me, Dylan, why should I, or any of those like me, care about the death of the king? The man was a *monster*."

"Cass," Dylan chided him with soft reproach, but it didn't sound like his heart was really in it. Standing just a few feet away, Tanya looked as though she agreed with the fae.

"His arrogance, his bloodlust, his intolerance of those who weren't his kind?" Cassiel was preaching to the choir, but it didn't seem to matter. There was a fire in his eyes that set Katerina's teeth on edge. A deep-seated hatred she was only beginning to understand. "It wouldn't have been long before he rounded up all the rest of us and had his soldiers finish what they started." His face tightened with rage and he stormed back towards the main street, only to whirl back around again—incensed beyond reason. "And don't even get me *started* on the prince—"

"The prince who's about to become the king?" Dylan interrupted fiercely.

For the second time, the alley went quiet. But while the others fumed and worried in silence, the princess was just starting to realize the key to her survival.

Cassiel didn't want to see her brother on the throne. Neither did Tanya. Neither did Dylan. Neither did the rest of the supernatural community, for that matter. The weight of her family blood may have hung like a curse over her head, but this one crucial fact could prove her only salvation.

The silence stretched on for longer than was bearable before breaking with a quiet question.

"You have the rightful claim?"

Katerina's head snapped up to see Cassiel's eyes burning into hers. She hated the way he was looking at her. Like he was trying to decide between the lesser of two evils. But on this point, at least, she was perfectly clear.

"Yes. I am."

There was something different about the way she said the words. A ringing sort of authority that echoed off the stones. The others lifted their heads, stared at her for a moment, then turned to the fae. Waiting for whatever came next.

But Cassiel had eyes only for Katerina. Staring so hard, it was like he was looking into her very soul. For a moment, he was unconvinced. Then his shoulders fell with an almost inaudible sigh. "What's your plan?"

Dylan let out a quick breath, unaware he'd been holding it in. His face cleared with a deep kind of relief before his lips curved up into a smile. "My plan was to find you."

There was a beat of silence.

"...and?"

Another beat.

"And hope you could come up with something better than 'try not to panic.'"

Katerina closed her eyes, resisting the urge to wrap her fingers around Dylan's neck. *I knew it. I knew he didn't have a plan.*

Cassiel shot him a look of sheer exasperation, running his hands back through his blond hair. His eyes lifted towards the horizon, lost in thought, before lightening with a sudden idea. "Brookfield Hall."

Just two simple words, but Katerina got the feeling they were going to change her life forever. At any rate, Dylan grabbed onto them like a life raft.

"You think that could work?" he asked quietly, not daring to hope.

Cassiel looked uncertain, then worried, then resigned. "It's the only chance we have. At least until we figure out the next step."

The four of them fell quiet for a moment before Tanya stomped her foot, her cinnamon hair quivering with impatience. "Does someone want to clue the rest of us in? Like *now*?"

Cassiel glanced over with a faint grin, while Dylan rolled his eyes.

"Brookfield Hall is a safe house we used to have in the mountains. It's a long way from here, but it's completely off the grid. No matter how many people might be hunting you, they'll never make it all the way to Brookfield. You'll be safe."

"For a *while*," Cassiel clarified. Katerina got the feeling the guy wasn't exactly the 'glass half-full' type. "You'll be safe for a *while*, until we figure out what the heck we're going to do next."

The others shared a quick glance, more worried than they were letting on, then Tanya flipped back her hair and set off towards the street with a confident smile.

"To Brookfield, then. We'll get there in one piece, or die trying."

"That's the spirit," Cassiel echoed, following along behind. "One day at a time."

Katerina stared after them with wide eyes, shaking her head in disbelief. "You guys have *got* to learn to give a better pep talk—"

She took a step to follow them but a hand shot out of nowhere, pulling her back. She glanced back in surprise to see Dylan standing right behind her, staring down into her eyes.

"Is this all right?" he asked softly. "The four of us. Is this something you want?"

She pulled back a few inches in surprise. "Do I have a choice?"

His face tightened with concern, and he slowly shook his head. "No, I don't think so."

She absorbed this silently, trying not to look as frightened as she felt. "Is the fae going to kill me in my sleep?"

He shook his head much faster this time. "No, he'd make sure you were awake."

"Oh, well, that's comforting." Katerina glanced up again, forcing a smile. A trick she'd learned from him. "Then it's the four of us. Four of us against the world."

There was a heavy pause. One that got even heavier by the second.

"...don't say it like that."

Katerina stifled a shudder, hurrying after him towards the street.

"Yeah, it sounded better in my head."

Chapter 12

THEY SPENT THE NIGHT in Lakewood, moving to a different inn on the other side of the village. The last thing they wanted was to explain to the proprietor of the first one why it was covered in blood, and according to the two men the four of them were going to need all the rest they could get before starting out on the long journey to Brookfield the following morning.

It was through the Black Forest and over the Calabrace Mountains. These were words that meant very little to Katerina, but she was quickly learning to base her reactions off the reactions of those around her. If they were worried, so was she. If they were resting, she would do the same.

"So do you think they're going to be okay in there?" Katerina slipped under the covers of her cot, tilting her head towards the wall. "Or do you think they'll kill each other in the night?"

For one night only, she and Tanya were sharing a room while Dylan and Cassiel were right next door. From tomorrow on, they'd all be sleeping under the same tent. But, given that it was their last night in civilization, they felt a certain level of propriety was in order.

Tanya followed her gaze then slipped into her own bed, pulling the covers up with a grin. "They'll fight for sure. And I like Dylan, but I hope the fae wins." Her eyes took on a dreamy sort of hue. "I could stare at him for the rest of eternity."

Katerina snorted with laughter, imagining the mayhem just beyond the wall. "I think he could stare at *himself* for the rest of eternity."

"Yeah...but that's probably his only fault."

The two girls shared a look, erupting into a sudden fit of giggles. A fit that soon escalated to the point where neither one was able to stop.

As strange as the situation was for Katerina, running for her life with a bunch of strangers through the twists and turns of a magical world, it was just as strange for Tanya. Her entire life, the girl had been alone. Her entire life, she'd been drifting from one town to the next. Always with a different identity. Always with an expiration date before she'd have to move on.

In a way, this impromptu sleepover—two teenage girls nestled beneath the covers, laughing at the plight of their friends—was the most normal, yet completely absurd, part of the journey yet.

They laughed and laughed and laughed, then abruptly grew shy. The room fell quiet, but the smiles lingered on their faces as the beginnings of a tentative friendship were made.

"Thank you," Tanya said suddenly, in a voice most unlike her own. "Thank you for letting me come with you."

Their eyes met, and Katerina's entire face warmed with a smile. "Thank you for coming."

Those were the last words they said until morning, but things were different the next day when they awoke. They were a little easier. They were a little more familiar. They were a hopeful beginning to the start of many things to come.

The men had slightly different luck.

"Seven hells!" Dylan angrily shook out his dark hair as the two emerged from the room the next morning and joined the girls outside. "I forgot what a nightmare you are to room with."

The girls shared a giggle, but Cassiel was unfazed.

"If by a *nightmare*, you mean that I refuse to 'keep watch' until four in the morning with the lights on and the window down...then, yeah. I guess I'm a nightmare."

"Completely unreasonable," Dylan muttered as the fae pushed past him on the way to get some breakfast. "You'd think I was asking a lot."

Katerina was unable to tell whether or not he was joking, so she wisely chose to move on.

"What's on the agenda for the morning?" she asked brightly, determined to make the most of their trip no matter how dangerous it might be. "Breakfast, then we head out?"

Cassiel shook his head, finishing off an apple as Dylan tossed back a swig of cider.

"No, we have to stock up on some supplies first," he replied. "Brookfield is completely off the grid—that's the whole point. It means we won't be able to get the things we need; we'll have to bring them with us."

The things we need? But we've been living off the land for over a month now.

The princess shook her head in confusion, trying to understand. "What kinds of things?"

"Booze," the men answered at the same time.

It was the only thing they'd agreed upon since meeting. They flashed each other a matching scowl, then headed off in separate directions to search the town. They'd almost disappeared completely, when Dylan doubled back, grabbing Katerina by the arm.

"Stay right by Tanya, do you understand?" He bent down, forcing her to meet his gaze. "*Right* by her. Swear it."

"All right, all right. I swear." Katerina yanked her arm away, rubbing it with a petulant glare. "You're pretty flippin' handsy, you know that? Especially considering I outrank you by about ten thousand degrees."

His eyebrows shot up with an amused smile. "Pulling rank, are we?" She shrugged testily and he flashed another grin. "Well, you didn't seem to mind all the times I was handsy before."

What?!

As Tanya graciously excused herself, muttering something about 'having to walk her dog,' Katerina turned to Dylan in shock, hardly able to believe her own ears. "Excuse me?"

The grin never faltered. If anything, it only got wider.

"Saving you from the goblins, pulling you out of that ghost..." he prompted, making no effort to hide his smile. "What did you think I meant?"

Katerina didn't know how to respond. Not only was she completely baffled as to whether or not he was teasing, but she had absolutely no experience either way. Flirting wasn't something that was really done in the castle. Not with the princess, at least. And, yes, she'd occasionally giggled and gossiped with her ladies when a particularly fine man came to court, but giggling and gossiping was the end of it. There was never any direct contact. Let alone flirting.

Unless...he wasn't flirting. Unless...he was just making a joke.

Her senses abandoned her completely and she stood, pale and helpless, for so long that Dylan eventually took pity on her. He rolled his eyes, then pulled her in for a one-armed hug.

"Relax, Princess." His lips brushed her hair and tickled the top of her ear as he whispered. "I promise I'll keep my hands to myself in the future."

Without another word, he left her standing in the middle of the street. Wondering what the heck just happened. Wondering if she'd made things better or worse. Certain of only a single thing.

For better or worse, something had just changed between them.

"Tanya?"

The second she called the shifter's name, the girl appeared by her side. She should have known. There was no way Dylan would have walked away unless she was nearby. With as much grace and dignity as she could muster, she flashed the girl a tight smile and gestured to the shops.

"Are we supposed to be getting booze, too? You know, I don't have any money."

Tanya let out a wild giggle. The kind that startled, but made one smile at the same time. "A princess with no money. That's just the funniest thing I've ever heard."

Katerina's smile faded into something rather dry. "Oh, yeah? What about a girl who spent a significant portion of the last few months travelling around as a goblin?"

The giggling stopped abruptly.

"Touché."

They steered the conversation wisely in another direction, and wandered further up the road.

"At any rate—no. We don't need to get any more booze." Tanya flipped her hair over her shoulder, her bright eyes scanning down the street. "Between the two of them, I'm sure Dylan and Cass will come back with enough to sate an army. What we might need are medical supplies."

There was nothing particularly ominous about the way she said it. Nothing about her tone that would clue one in to trouble. It was the principle of the thing.

Of course we will. Because what are the odds of getting out of this unscathed?

The shifter correctly interpreted the look on her face, and quickly flashed her a reassuring smile. "It's no big deal—really. Standard practice whenever you go on a long trip. Between the four of us, I'm sure we're going to be fine."

"Right." Katerina nodded quickly. "We're going to be fine."

Except the entire royal army is after us, my beloved giant saw tracks of theirs in the woods, and for all I know my brother's hell hounds are already on my trail.

But, yeah—I'm sure we'll be fine.

It was a lie at the worst, a pipe dream at the best. But either way, the girls were content to let it go and get on with the rest of their day. There was only so long you could stay in a state of abject terror and misery before bits of light started slipping through the cracks.

"So where do we get medical supplies in a place like this?" Katerina asked, faking a great deal more confidence than she actually felt.

Tanya flashed her a grin, seeing through the effort with ease. "We get them from a witch, of course. Come on. I spotted a coven by the fountain yesterday afternoon."

A coven?! Of witches?!

For the second time in less than a minute Katerina flashed a deceptively confident smile, and gestured to the road ahead. "Lead the way."

THE WITCHES WERE ABSOLUTELY nothing like what Katerina had expected. She had conjured up an image of a female version of Alwyn. Stately. Refined. Wrinkled with dignity and old age. What she found was a group of cackling, haggling, abrasive young women. Frizzy hair and fraying clothes, with a bucket-load of neurotic superstitions to boot.

First, they didn't have what the girls were looking for. Then they might have it, but they were unsure as to the price. Then they had definitely found it, but wanted to know what the girls would be willing to pay before they admitted its original cost.

'Round and 'round they went, straining everyone's patience. After only a few minutes Tanya was already at her wit's end, and when one of the witches demand that Katerina leave the tent because she 'didn't trust people with red hair' the princess couldn't get out the door fast enough.

"Do not leave me with these people," Tanya commanded through gritted teeth.

Katerina merely clapped her on the shoulder and slipped away with a smile. "I'll be right outside. In the meantime, you should shift into one of them. Add to the confusion."

Her smile was rewarded with a sarcastic glare.

"That's hilarious. Who knew royalty was so flippin' hilarious."

It looked like she wanted to say plenty more, but before she could get the chance Katerina slipped outside, breathing in gulps of fresh hair as if she'd been trapped underwater. The witches had an unhealthy obsession with incense, and she didn't realize how much it was messing with her head until she got back into the open breeze. The music was playing, the flowers were blowing gently in the breeze, and before Katerina realized what she was doing she began drifting along with the crowd. Smiling at the children playing on the grass and peering curiously into the shops.

She didn't go far. She had made a promise, after all. But just as she was turning around to head back to the shops, a little whimper caught her ear.

She scanned the crowd for the source of the noise, her gaze falling on a little boy, crouched by the side of the road. There were tears on his face and dirt on his knees, but despite the fact that he was openly weeping no one else stopped to pay him any notice.

"Sweetheart?" she called, weaving her way desperately through the crowd. "Sweetheart, what's the matter?"

The boy looked up with a start, then bolted the second she got close. He appeared to be limping, and cast a frightened glance over his shoulder as he scampered up the grassy hill and away from the festival, disappearing into the trees.

Katerina paused at the edge of the road, staring at the woods with a look of tortured indecision. Twice, she stopped one of the people around her, asking if they would help her find the boy. Twice she was either propositioned or ignored.

She was about to hurry back to the witches and get Tanya for help, when another little cry drifted up out of the forest. This one was even more plaintive than the first. A chill of dread stole through her chest and she ran towards it without thinking, losing herself in the thick woods.

"Hello?" she called, searching frantically for a little boy in a sea of green. She could still hear the crying, but somehow the child had vanished into the trees. "Can you hear me? Please, don't be afraid. I only want to help. Are you hungry? Would you like some food—"

A heavy boot caught her right in the stomach, doubling her over where she stood. A second kick and she went flying through the air, landing with a sharp crack on the forest floor.

Pain, the likes of which she'd never felt, radiated down from her head as the world in front of her flickered on and off. She could just barely make out the outlines of three people standing in front of her. Two were very tall. One was exceedingly small.

"That was even easier than I thought," a gruff voice burst out laughing, starling the smaller figure by his side. "You did well. Now take your coins and go."

A handful of gold rained down on the leaves in front of Katerina's face. She blinked at them in a daze, trying to focus, when a pair of little hands scooped them up. She lifted her head just long enough to connect with a set of dark eyes. A child's eyes. No tears on his face now.

The boy met her gaze for a split second before whispering, "I'm sorry," then he took off into the trees. She stared after him in shock, blinking what felt like blood from her eyes, when a sudden shadow fell over her crumpled form.

"Doesn't look much like a princess." One of the men put his hands on his knees, cocking his head to shamelessly look her up and down. "Are you sure we got the right one?"

"I'm sure." The first man reached down and ripped off her cloak in one, sudden movement, spilling her crimson hair all over the forest floor. "I actually saw her once at the castle at the St. Martin's Day feast. It's her, all right. I could never forget such a pretty face."

The two men chuckled darkly, glancing around the woods. Katerina didn't know what was different, but there was a sudden change in the air. An anxious sort of tension that wasn't there before.

"We're the only ones out here, right?" the second man asked nervously. "The others headed up towards Banff?"

The first man nodded silently, staring down at the fallen princess with a hungry gleam in his eyes. "It's just you and me. And her. And we've got nothing but time..."

Katerina didn't understand what was happening as they dragged her through the underbrush and propped her up against the base of a tree. She didn't understand why they weren't binding her hands, preparing to take her back to their leader. For that matter, she didn't understand why they were so nervous all of a sudden. She was the one about to be taken back in chains.

Unless I can tell them the truth. Unless I can tell them what really happened.

"You're making a mistake," she mumbled, still trying to clear her throbbing head. "My brother set this whole thing up. He killed the—"

A gloved hand swung out of nowhere, slapping her in the face. The world went dim again, then came back only in muted colors as the men talked amongst themselves.

"Just be quick about it." The second man stood with his back to her, anxiously peering out over the trees. "Once is enough. Then it's my turn."

...his turn?

The first man knelt right in front of her, stroking the side of her face, a wicked smile on his lips. "I'll take my time, thank you very much. It isn't often you get to see a princess, let alone—"

A blistering growl cut through the air. A growl so wild and savage, it pierced through Katerina's bloodshot fog and roused her from the inevitable sleep.

"What was that?" the second man gasped, clutching the hilt of his blade. "Did you hear—"

Another growl and the men came together with a shout, standing back to back with weapons drawn as they looked out over the trees. Katerina's eyes opened wide, but they seemed to have forgotten all about her. Whatever was coming, they would surely not lift a finger in her defense—not when she was already marked for death. Or for a fate much, much worse.

She tried desperately to scream, but her tongue was glued to the roof of her mouth. She tried to bring her knees up to her chest, but her legs were palsied and weak. In the end, she could only sit there. Staring in terror at the wilderness beyond. Waiting for whatever monster had made that blood-curdling sound to come and finish her off.

"I think it's gone." The man who'd slapped her across the face lowered his sword a fraction of an inch. "Maybe we scared it off—"

As if to answer, another growl echoed through the trees. This one almost seemed to be laughing. For a second, the entire clearing stood still. The air quivered and even the birds paused in their song. Then the leaves parted and out stepped the biggest wolf Katerina had ever seen.

She let out a quiet gasp, freezing perfectly still.

Massive didn't even begin to cover it. The thing was enormous. Well over two hundred pounds of solid, weather-hardened muscle. Its deadly claws pawed aggressively into the ground, and even from where she sat Katerina could see two glistening rows of razor-sharp teeth.

Most people would have fainted. Those who didn't would have run away. But in Katerina's semi-concussed state, she could think of only one thing to say.

"...you're beautiful."

The men shot her a look of utter astonishment, and even the wolf turned its head to gaze her way. Its blue eyes locked onto hers as the wind rippled through its chocolate fur.

It might have been a strange thing to say, but it was undeniably true. There was a grace and power to the animal, even in stillness. A commanding sort of presence that brought the rest of the forest to its knees. She had never seen one so close before, not a live one anyway, and despite the fact that she was surely about to die she couldn't help but stare. There was something so familiar about it, yet foreign at the same time. As if she'd spotted it once from the road without realizing. Seen its face without remembering when or why.

A metallic hiss sliced through the air, bringing her back to the present; the two soldiers advanced at the same time. While the beast was clearly as frightening as it sounded, they still outnumbered it two-to-one. And they still had their swords.

Katerina's heart pounded in her chest as they closed in on the animal, raising those swords at the same time. She'd seen enough soldiers in her day to know that the men were well-trained, and she'd seen enough bloodshed not to want to see any more of it now.

Run! Tears rolled down her face as she stared at the beautiful wolf, wishing desperately she could make it understand. *They'll kill you—please run!*

If she didn't know better, she could have sworn the animal heard her. It turned its head again, meeting her eyes for a fleeting moment, before its shoulders fell with a frustrated sigh.

It was the sigh that caught Katerina's attention. It was the sigh that brought her back to life.

"Dylan?"

Before anyone had a chance to reply, the forest sprang into action. One second, the wolf was standing in the clearing. Deceptively still. Facing off against the two men. The next, it was flying through the air, moving at a near blinding speed as it hurled its body straight at Katerina's attackers.

She let out a scream as the glint of two swords flashed through the air, clashing together with a sickening clang. There was a splash of blood, followed by a high-pitched scream. But it was a human scream. Not a wolf's. The man who'd been standing guard in front of her fell to his knees, dropping his sword and clutching his savaged shoulder as blood streamed over his fingers. His friend darted forward to help him, but by that time it was too late.

There was a flash of dark fur, followed by another stricken cry. A cry that cut off in a gurgle of blood as the wolf sank its teeth deep into the man's throat.

"Thomas!"

The first man—the one who'd slapped her, the one who proudly insisted upon taking his time—abandoned form altogether and ran full-speed towards the animal. It was a bold strategy, but it proved to be a fatal mistake. He was expecting the wolf to act like a wolf. He was expecting it to either run off in surprise or fiercely protect its kill. But the wolf did neither of these things. As the man sprinted towards it, it sprinted at lightning speed right back towards the man.

They met in the center of the clearing with a sickening clash. Metal on bone. Teeth against blade. For a split second, they were moving too fast for Katerina to see what had happened. Then a crimson spray rained across the leaves.

She pulled in a breathless gasp, peering through the cracks in her fingers to see which one had come out on top. She knew who she *should* be hoping for, but when the dust finally cleared her heart warmed at the very sight of the wolf.

It was standing atop the man's chest, its sharp claws buried deep in his flesh. There was a streak of blood across its nose, but it didn't seem to notice. It had eyes only for the princess.

She froze very still as they locked eyes, staring across the bloody clearing. For a moment, neither of them moved. Then, without ever breaking her gaze, the wolf leapt off the man's broken body, buried its teeth in his shoulder, and dragged him back off into the trees.

What happened next was something Katerina would never forget. Something she swore she'd remember for as long as she lived. She couldn't see it, but she could hear it well enough. The snap of every breaking bone. The tear of every piece of skin. The pitiful screams that faded, then eventually died—replaced only with the low, rumbling growls of the wolf.

It didn't take very long. That's the thing that struck her most. It didn't take long for men to die. When it was finished the wolf walked back into the clearing, its chocolate fur dripping with a fresh layer of crimson blood.

She should have been afraid, but she wasn't. She should have been trying to run, but all she did was hold out her hand. The wolf stared at it for a moment before bowing its head with an unmistakable sigh and walking slowly across the clearing.

It came to a stop a few feet away, just beyond the reach of her fingers. She tried to stretch another inch more, but it was no use. In the end, she merely stared up into its eyes.

"Please?"

It waited for a moment. Watching. Thinking. Debating. Then it took a step closer.

Katerina's face lit up with a wondrous smile as her fingertips grazed the soft waves of chocolate fur. She moved cautiously at first, then with unrestrained delight. Burying her hands in the sides of its neck. Feeling the strong muscles beneath the glossy coat of fur. Letting its smoky, woodsy scent wash over her as she moved herself up higher and reached for its face.

But at that point the wolf pulled back, eyeing her hand uncertainly. She froze perfectly still, not daring to move, tilting her head with a little smile.

"Please?" she asked again. "I promise I won't hurt you."

Hurt YOU?

In hindsight, it seemed like a very stupid thing to say. The wolf apparently agreed, because it actually rolled its eyes before taking a step closer. As she hesitantly reached up between them, it lowered its giant head, pressing the side of its face against her palm.

It was unlike anything she'd ever felt before.

Her breath caught in her chest as she stared deep into its eyes. Blue eyes. Eyes the exact color of the morning sky. A sudden wave of emotion rushed over her, and without stopping to think she lifted to her knees and planted the softest kiss on its cheek.

"Dylan, is that you?"

The wolf met her eyes for the briefest moment before dropping its head with yet another frustrated sigh. A sigh that Katerina had heard many times before. A sigh that promised a furious lecture soon to come.

Her entire face warmed as she shakily pushed to her feet. The corners of her lips curved upward. "Dylan. I know it's you."

She nodded, the grin turning into a smile. *Looks like I'm not the only one with a secret...*

To Be Continued...

EVERLASTING...
Coming February 2018

BOOK 2 OF THE QUEEN'S Alpha Series

When the crown prince puts a bounty on her head, Katerina and her gang of misfits find themselves facing trouble at every turn. It's a race to get to the safe house in time, but will they pull together to work as a team or will their differences pull them apart?

Strengths and weaknesses are put to the test as Katerina is plunged headfirst into a magical world she never knew existed. Fiction becomes reality as the characters from her childhood fairytales come to life, bringing with them secrets she could never have imagined.

Her bloodline gives her the right to call herself their queen, but is the division between the royal family and the magical kingdom too great? How can she mend the damage of the past?

More importantly...can she be the one to unite her people?

Find W.J. May

Website:
http://www.wanitamay.yolasite.com
Facebook:
https://www.facebook.com/pages/Author-WJ-May-FAN-PAGE/141170442608149
Newsletter:
SIGN UP FOR W.J. May's Newsletter to find out about new releases, updates, cover reveals and even freebies!
http://eepurl.com/97aYf

More books by W.J. May

The Chronicles of Kerrigan

BOOK I - *Rae of Hope* is FREE!
   Book Trailer:
   http://www.youtube.com/watch?v=gILAwXxx8MU
   Book II - *Dark Nebula*
   Book Trailer:
   http://www.youtube.com/watch?v=Ca24STi_bFM
   Book III - *House of Cards*
   Book IV - *Royal Tea*
   Book V - *Under Fire*
   Book VI - *End in Sight*
   Book VII – *Hidden Darkness*
   Book VIII – *Twisted Together*
   Book IX – *Mark of Fate*
   Book X – *Strength & Power*
   Book XI – *Last One Standing*
   BOOK XII – *Rae of Light*

PREQUEL –
    Christmas Before the Magic
    Question the Darkness
    Into the Darkness
    Fight the Darkness
    Alone the Darkness
    Lost the Darkness

SEQUEL –
    Matter of Time
    Time Piece
    Second Chance
    Glitch in Time
    Our Time
    Precious Time

Hidden Secrets Saga:
Download Seventh Mark part 1 For FREE
Book Trailer:
http://www.youtube.com/watch?v=Y-_yVYC1gvo

LIKE MOST TEENAGERS, Rouge is trying to figure out who she is and what she wants to be. With little knowledge about her past, she has questions but has never tried to find the answers. Everything changes when she befriends a strangely intoxicating family. Siblings Grace and Michael, appear to have secrets which seem connected to Rouge. Her hunch is confirmed when a horrible incident occurs at an outdoor party. Rouge may be the only one who can find the answer.

An ancient journal, a Sioghra necklace and a special mark force life-altering decisions for a girl who grew up unprepared to fight for her life or others.

All secrets have a cost and Rouge's determination to find the truth can only lead to trouble...or something even more sinister.

RADIUM HALOS - THE SENSELESS SERIES
Book 1 is FREE:

Everyone needs to be a hero at one point in their life.

The small town of Elliot Lake will never be the same again.

Caught in a sudden thunderstorm, Zoe, a high school senior from Elliot Lake, and five of her friends take shelter in an abandoned uranium mine. Over the next few days, Zoe's hearing sharpens drastically, beyond what any normal human being can detect. She tells her friends, only to learn that four others have an increased sense as well. Only Kieran, the new boy from Scotland, isn't affected.

Fashioning themselves into superheroes, the group tries to stop the strange occurrences happening in their little town. Muggings, break-ins, disappearances, and murder begin to hit too close to home. It leads the team to think someone knows about their secret - someone who wants them all dead.

An incredulous group of heroes. A traitor in the midst. Some dreams are written in blood.

Courage Runs Red
The Blood Red Series
Book 1 is FREE

WHAT IF COURAGE WAS your only option?

When Kallie lands a college interview with the city's new hot-shot police officer, she has no idea everything in her life is about to change. The detective is young, handsome and seems to have an unnatural ability to stop the increasing local crime rate. Detective Liam's particular interest in Kallie sends her heart and head stumbling over each other.

When a raging blood feud between vampires spills into her home, Kallie gets caught in the middle. Torn between love and family loyalty she must find the courage to fight what she fears the most and possibly risk everything, even if it means dying for those she loves.

Daughter of Darkness

Victoria[1]

Only Death Could Stop Her Now

The Daughters of Darkness is a series of female heroines who may or may not know each other, but all have the same father, Vlad Montour.

Victoria is a Hunter Vampire

---

1. http://www.amazon.com/gp/product/B0102ZNSQK/
   ref=as_li_qf_sp_asin_il_tl?ie=UTF8&camp=1789&creative=9325&cre-
   ativeASIN=B0102ZNSQK&linkCode=as2&tag=lextim-20&linkId=TO4WGCMP-
   WX4SOL6D

Don't miss out!

Click the button below and you can sign up to receive emails whenever W.J. May publishes a new book. There's no charge and no obligation.

https://books2read.com/r/B-A-SSF-ZBQQ

BOOKS 2 READ

Connecting independent readers to independent writers.

Did you love *Eternal*? Then you should read *Never Look Back* by W.J. May!

USA Today Bestselling author, W.J. May, brings you to a new level of fantasy. Fans of Underworld and paranormal worlds will love this story!

"The wise learn many things from their enemies."

My name's Atlanta Skolar, and I'm a huntress. No, not the vampire-slaying type, or the ever-brooding Winchester brothers from *Supernatural*. I live a relatively normal life—during the day at least. I go to school, have friends, and try my best to survive Uncle James' horrendous cooking.

However, the nights in the city of Calen are not always calm. There's a thin veil between our world and the world of monsters, the good and the bad. I'm one of the few who stands between the two. With the help of my uncle, who's taken me in since my parents' deaths,

I spend the nights making sure the balance is maintained and that each side keeps to their respective places.

At least, that was until something rattled the cages and everything hit the fan. There's a new evil in town, an evil that's been here before, and it may be responsible for my parents' deaths. An evil that isn't satisfied with the balance. It'll do all it can to make sure darkness falls over Calen and the rest of the world once again.

Scary? That ain't the half of it.

It's particularly interested in me.

Why? No idea.

But it's my job as a huntress to make sure the evil is stopped, no matter what.

Also by W.J. May

Bit-Lit Series
Lost Vampire
Cost of Blood
Price of Death

Blood Red Series
Courage Runs Red
The Night Watch
Marked by Courage
Forever Night

Daughters of Darkness: Victoria's Journey
Victoria
Huntress
Coveted (A Vampire & Paranormal Romance)
Twisted

Hidden Secrets Saga

Seventh Mark - Part 1
Seventh Mark - Part 2
Marked By Destiny
Compelled
Fate's Intervention
Chosen Three
The Hidden Secrets Saga: The Complete Series

Paranormal Huntress Series
Never Look Back
Coven Master
Alpha's Permission

Prophecy Series
Only the Beginning
White Winter
Secrets of Destiny

The Chronicles of Kerrigan
Rae of Hope
Dark Nebula
House of Cards
Royal Tea
Under Fire
End in Sight
Hidden Darkness
Twisted Together
Mark of Fate

Strength & Power
Last One Standing
Rae of Light
The Chronicles of Kerrigan Box Set Books # 1 - 6

The Chronicles of Kerrigan: Gabriel
Living in the Past
Staring at the Future
Present For Today

The Chronicles of Kerrigan Prequel
Question the Darkness
Into the Darkness
Fight the Darkness
Alone in the Darkness
Lost in Darkness
Christmas Before the Magic
The Chronicles of Kerrigan Prequel Series Books #1-3

The Chronicles of Kerrigan Sequel
A Matter of Time
Time Piece
Second Chance
Glitch in Time
Our Time
Precious Time

The Hidden Secrets Saga
Seventh Mark (part 1 & 2)

The Queen's Alpha Series
Eternal

The Senseless Series
Radium Halos
Radium Halos - Part 2
Nonsense

Standalone
Shadow of Doubt (Part 1 & 2)
Five Shades of Fantasy
Shadow of Doubt - Part 1
Shadow of Doubt - Part 2
Four and a Half Shades of Fantasy
Dream Fighter
What Creeps in the Night
Forest of the Forbidden
HuNted
Arcane Forest: A Fantasy Anthology
Ancient Blood of the Vampire and Werewolf

Made in the USA
Monee, IL
16 October 2020